ALL THE WRONG QUESTIONS

———

"Who Could That Be at This Hour?"
"When Did You See Her Last?"
"Shouldn't You Be in School?"

ADDITIONAL REPORTS

———

File Under: 13 Suspicious Incidents

ALL THE WRONG QUESTIONS

?

3

"Shouldn't You Be in School?"

LEMONY SNICKET

ART BY SETH

Little, Brown and Company

New York Boston

Little, Brown and Company

Hachette Book Group
237 Park Avenue, New York, NY 10017
Visit our website at lb-kids.com

Little, Brown and Company is a division of Hachette Book Group, Inc. The Little, Brown name and logo are trademarks of Hachette Book Group, Inc.

The publisher is not responsible for websites (or their content) that are not owned by the publisher.

First Edition: September 2014

Library of Congress Control Number: 2014933203

ISBN 978-0-316-12306-8

10 9 8 7 6 5 4 3 2 1

RRD-C

Printed in the United States of America

CHAPTER ONE

There was a town, and there was a librarian,
and there was a fire. While I was in town I was
hired to investigate this fire, and I thought the
librarian could help me bring a villain to justice. I
was almost thirteen and I was wrong. I was wrong
about all of it. I should have asked the question
"Why would someone destroy one building when
they really wanted to destroy another?" Instead,
I asked the wrong questions—four wrong questions, more or less. This is the account of the third.

I was spending a bad morning in a good library. What was bad was the weather, which was unforgivably hot. The sun was having a tantrum so fierce that all the shade had been scared away, and the sidewalks of Stain'd-by-the-Sea, the town in which I had been spending my time, were no place for a decent person to walk. The library, with its calm and cooling silence, was the only comfortable place to spend the early hours of the day.

The weather wasn't the only thing that made the morning bad. There was a man, a vicious villain who went by the name of Hangfire. Every morning that found Hangfire still at large was a bad morning. He was hiding somewhere in town, biding his sinister time and planning his troublesome plans, and hiding and planning with him were his associates in an organization called the Inhumane Society. Recently they had set up shop in the Colophon Clinic, if the phrase "set up shop" can mean "turn an empty hospital into a place where many children could be kept prisoner for some sinister purpose." Although the Colophon Clinic had been destroyed, I was certain Hangfire was looking for a new location for whatever plot he was cooking up.

For this reason I'd taken to spending my afternoons watching over the town's only remaining school. I guess I was watching to see if any children were being abducted. They weren't, not by Hangfire or anyone else. Most of them were already gone. The ink industry, which had once been the pride of Stain'd-by-the-Sea, had faded away, and most of the town had faded along with it. Stain'd Secondary had a large campus, a phrase which here meant that there was a tall, wide building that curved slightly like a seashell— the auditorium perhaps, or the gymnasium— with a grouping of small buildings in its shadow. Once the campus must have been a loud and busy place when the buzzer signaled the end of the day. Now it was much too large for the

3

handful of students who walked quietly out into the gray afternoon. Some of them looked familiar from my time in town. Some of them didn't. All of them looked tired and none of them met my eyes. It was lonely work to watch over them, but I didn't learn anything about Hangfire's dark scheme.

I hoped I'd have better luck in the library, and on that bad morning I was reading two things I hoped would help. The first was a book on caviar, and I didn't care who knew it. Caviar is the eggs of a fish, usually a sturgeon, black and shiny and served on small pieces of toast at parties to which you are not invited. As of that morning, at thirteen years of age, I'd never eaten any. I was not interested in eating any. I was reading *Caviar: Salty Jewel of the Tasty Sea* in the hopes of learning something, but as I finished a paragraph about the special tanks they use when the sturgeon are young, I wondered if I was wrong once more.

The other thing I was reading was a secret. It had taken ten days to reach me, through the hard work of a number of people close to my heart but far away on the map. We'd learned together, in what most people would call a history class, that one good way to hide things is in plain sight. People often forget to look at something right in front of them, and as promised I had found something taped to the underside of the table where I always sat. It had been tricky to peel away the tape without anyone noticing, and once it was removed from its hiding place and smoothed out so it would be easier to read, I kept sliding it under the book on caviar whenever I feared I was being watched.

It was silly to hide it. It was just a small newspaper article from the city. Nobody in Stain'd-by-the-Sea cared about it. Nobody but me.

I hid it anyway, when the librarian approached. You cannot have a really terrific library without at least one terrific librarian, the way you cannot have a really terrific bedroom unless you can lock the door. Stain'd-by-the-Sea's only librarian—or, as he called himself, sub-librarian—was terrific because he was kind and helpful without being irritating or bossy. This sort of person is an endangered species, almost extinct. Spending time in his library was like seeing a rare and strange beast that I might not ever see again, and sure enough, in a few short days this library, the only one in Stain'd-by-the-Sea, would be gone forever.

"I'm sorry to interrupt you, Snicket," the librarian said, in his very deep voice. His name was Dashiell Qwerty, a tidy and proper name that didn't match his appearance. As usual, he was wearing a leather jacket decorated with small scraps of metal, a garment so dangerous-looking that Qwerty's hair always seemed to be scurrying away from it. I don't know what a matching name might have been. Wildhairy Oddjacket comes to mind.

"That's quite all right," I said, and heard

the newspaper rustle underneath my book. The article told the story of a young woman who had been arrested in the city for the crime of breaking and entering. Breaking and entering wasn't the right term, I thought. My sister didn't break in, not really. She had simply entered the Museum of Items when the museum was closed. It didn't seem like a good reason to put someone in prison, but according to the article that was likely to happen.

"I was just checking to see if you had found everything you need," Qwerty said, either not noticing or pretending not to notice what I was hiding. "There are some new Italian dictionaries that I thought you might find interesting."

"Maybe another time," I said. "Right now I have just the book I'm looking for. I'm glad to see that the shelves are in order again."

"Yes, it was a bother to reorganize everything," Qwerty said, "but now the sprinkler and alarm system is finally installed. The controls are right over there in the northeast corner of the room, so I feel much less nervous about the threats that have been made."

"You've mentioned those threats before," I said, "but you've never said anything more about them."

"Yes, I have," Qwerty agreed, with a glance at the article in my lap, "and no, I haven't."

He looked at me and I looked at him. We both wanted to know each other's secrets, and we both wanted the other person to go first. This is something that happens quite a bit, which is why you so often see children and adults staring at one another in nervous silence. We might have stayed there for quite a long time, but a moth flew into Qwerty's line of sight and he swatted at it with a checkered handkerchief. Qwerty was a predator of the moth known as the Farnsworth Pulpeater, as the Farnsworth Pulpeater is a predator of paper. It appeared to be a battle that was to go on for quite some time without Qwerty or the moths giving up.

"Well, if you're content," Qwerty said, as a moth escaped his attack, "I'll excuse myself and let you be. That young woman looks like she might need my help."

I stood up too quickly. Even when reading two things at once, I had been thinking of something else entirely. The something else was a girl, taller than I was or older than I was or both. She had curious eyebrows, curved and coiled like question marks, and she had a smile that might have meant anything. Her eyes were green and her hair so black it made caviar look beige, and in her possession was a statue that was blacker still. The statue was of a mythical creature called the Bombinating Beast, and it gazed out through hollow, wicked eyes at all the trouble gathered around it. The girl's father was in trouble, captured by Hangfire, and she had tried to save him

9

by doing favors for the Inhumane Society, so now she was in trouble too. I had promised to help her, but I hadn't seen the girl or the statue in quite some time. The girl, and the promise I'd made, hovered in my head no matter what I was reading, and her name hovered in my ears like the song she played on an old-fashioned phonograph, and on a music box that her father had left behind. I didn't know what the song was, but I liked it.

Ellington Feint. Ellington Feint. Ellington Feint.

It's probably not her, I told myself, as I hurried to the entrance of the library, and it wasn't. It was Moxie Mallahan, a fine journalist and a good friend, with a hat that looked like a lowercase *a* and a typewriter in its own folding case that could type *a* and all the other letters. She put the case down with a small frown of pain. Her arm was still bandaged from a recent encounter with someone good with a knife.

"What's the news, Moxie?" I said.

"It's good to see you, Snicket," she replied. "You're not too busy doing whatever it is you're doing?"

"I always have time for an associate," I said. I led her back to my table, carrying her type-writer case. Her injury was partially my fault, as you can read in an account of mine. You don't have to read about it. I'm sure you have your own troubles.

"I've been looking through the archives of *The Stain'd Lighthouse*, like you asked me to," Moxie said, sitting down across from me. "It was boring work, Snicket."

"I'm sure it was," I said. *The Stain'd Lighthouse* was a newspaper that had once been at the break-fast table of every resident of Stain'd-by-the-Sea, thanks to the hard work of Moxie's family. But now the newspaper had folded, a term Moxie had explained to me. It did not mean folded the way you can fold a newspaper into a hat or a boat or a man with a sword riding on a swan. It meant that it had surrendered to the ink shortages that had scared so many of the town's citizens away. Moxie was the only journalist left in Stain'd-by-the-Sea, and the only thing left of the newspaper was vast piles of past editions, strewn around the rooms of the Mallahan lighthouse. "I'm sorry I had to ask you to do that," I said, "but I couldn't find anything in the library about Stain'd-by-the-Sea's fishing industry."

"I looked at the business section of the news-paper," Moxie said, "all the way back to before I was born. My mother used to say that the busi-ness section had all of the really exciting secrets hidden there in plain sight, but I'm not sure I found any. I wish she were still in town, so she would have been able to help me."

"I'm sure you'll hear from her soon," I said quickly, although I wasn't sure at all.

Moxie nodded, but she wasn't looking at me. She opened her typewriter case and looked at the page of notes she'd been typing. "The business section might have exciting secrets, but it's very boring to read."

"That's probably why they hide the secrets there."

"Maybe so. It was difficult to stay awake while I was reading it."

"Maybe you should have had some coffee."

"Not I, Snicket. I don't drink coffee. You're thinking of that girl who caused all the trouble with that statue."

"I guess I am thinking of her," I admitted. Ellington liked to sit at the counter of an establishment called Black Cat Coffee, on the corner of Caravan and Parfait. She often had her coffee very late at night and stayed there to watch the sun rise.

"Well, I wish you'd stop," Moxie said sourly. "Anyway, I found something that I thought you might think was helpful. It's from an article published when the town was arguing about draining the sea: 'Porter Roeman, who runs the Roe House, told reporters that he opposed the draining, as it would adversely affect local marine life.' What's 'adversely' mean?"

"Badly," I said, and we gave each other one grim nod each. Some years ago, the town had decided to drain the sea so the last few octopi could be found and harvested for ink. The idea was to save Ink Inc., which was Stain'd-by-the-Sea's largest and most important company. It was the wrong idea. The draining of the sea had drained the town along with it. The town's stores and restaurants had folded as quickly as *The Stain'd Lighthouse*. A fancy, top-drawer school on an island was now nothing but empty buildings on a pile of craggy rocks, connected by a bridge that was no longer necessary. Where once had been countless fish and swirling waves, there was now the Clusterous Forest, a vast, lawless landscape of shivering seaweed. And Ink Inc. had been affected as adversely as the rest of town, and had recently shut its doors for good. A young woman of my acquaintance, a brilliant chemist named Cleo Knight, was in a small cottage working on a solution to the ink problem, but I didn't know if she'd finish her work before the town disappeared completely. Nobody knew.

Moxie continued to read from her notes. "A successful fish business requires loyal workers and a steady supply of food. Mr. Roeman said that without a local source of plankton, Roe House would likely go out of business. And it did, Snicket. Stain'd-by-the-Sea's fishing industry is gone, just like everything else." She reached into her typewriter case and took out a photograph. "I developed this photograph myself, in the basement darkroom. It's Roe House on its last day of business. Feast your eyes, Snicket."

My eyes tried to feast but they nearly starved. The photograph showed a large, empty room, with small rectangular marks on the scuffed floor. In the far corner of the room was a small door, the only thing to look at. I looked at it. It could have led anywhere. A back room, I thought. An exit someplace. "It's a big room," I said finally.

Moxie looked at me. "Big enough to be Hangfire's new headquarters?"

"It doesn't look big enough to hold a large group of kidnapped children," I said, "but perhaps Hangfire has given up on that part of his plan."

"But what's the rest of his plan, Snicket?"

"I don't know," I admitted. "The Inhumane Society had all that aquatic equipment at the Colophon Clinic, so I thought the fishing indus-try might be involved somehow. But it doesn't seem like your search through the archives has turned up much."

"That's what I thought," Moxie said, and scratched at the bandage on her arm. She had told me to stop asking her if it still hurt. "But then I thought maybe we should go see for ourselves."

"Good idea."

"Come on, then. The address is 350 Way-ward Way."

"350 Wayward Way? I don't know where that is."

"Good thing you have an associate who grew up in this town," Moxie said with a smile. "Come on, Snicket. Stop lollygagging."

It is true that I was moving slowly, trying to figure out how to stand up and keep the news-paper article hidden at the same time. "I'll be with you in a moment," I said, using a phrase that rarely works.

Moxie cocked her head at me. "What *is* roe, anyway, Snicket?"

"Fish eggs," I said. "Caviar."

Moxie looked down at my reading. "So all this has to do with that book?"

"I'm not sure."

"Because I thought it might have to do with that newspaper article you're hiding under it."

"What newspaper article?"

17

"I'm a journalist, Snicket. You'll have to do better than that. Take out that newspaper article nice and slow, and don't use any cheap tricks to try and distract me."

"Fire! Fire!" The sudden cry almost made me drop the newspaper. I looked quickly around the library, as I'd been trained to do in such emergencies. Sprinkler system, I thought. Northeast corner. But without a compass, the phrase "northeast corner" might as well have been "I haven't the faintest idea."

"Help has arrived," I called. *"Where is the fire?"*

"There isn't one, Snicket," said the voice, familiar now. "I was just looking for you."

Moxie and I sighed, like we were both balloons pricked by the same needle, and down the aisle came the person who had deflated us. Part of my education required each apprentice to have a chaperone, and S. Theodora Markson was mine. The function of a chaperone is to serve as an example of the adult you might become, and Theodora served as a bad example. Her hair, for instance, was always a frightful mess, particularly when it was struggling against the leather helmet she seemed to enjoy wearing. She refused to tell me what the *S* stood for in her name, no matter how many times I asked her. But neither her hair nor her first name was the main problem with Theodora. I don't need to tell you what the problem is. You have met impossible people, and you know when you are stuck with them. They are of no more use than a heap of old boxes left in the middle of the sidewalk, but you end up tripping on them anyway.

"You're not supposed to scream fire in a library," I said, "unless you mean it."

"I wouldn't have had to scream," Theodora said, "if you'd left me a note saying where you were, as I specifically instructed."

"I did leave a note. It said I'd be at the library."

"Well, I didn't have time to read it all. We're in a hurry, Snicket. We have to stop screaming fire and investigate a case of arson."

"Arson?" Moxie said, rolling a new page into her typewriter. A suspicious fire was just the sort of thing that Moxie liked to write about.

My chaperone looked down at her and frowned. "Who are you?"

Moxie reached into the brim of her hat, which was where she kept printed cards stating her name and occupation. "We've met on a number of occasions," Moxie said, handing her one. "It's lovely to see you, Ms. Markson. Your apprentice was just returning a scrap of newspaper I lent him."

I frowned at Moxie while Theodora frowned at the card. "I believe this is *my* scrap of newspaper," I said, trying to sound dignified. "You must have left your scrap someplace else."

"Be sensible, Snicket," Theodora said. "We don't have time to fight over scraps. Give it to your playmate and let's go."

Moxie gave me a sly smile and held out her hand. I didn't want to give her the newspaper article, and I certainly didn't want to think of her as my playmate. But under Theodora's supervision I could not think what else to do. I surrendered the article, and in no time at all my sister's dilemma was folded up into a neat square and tucked into Moxie's hat.

"Maybe later," Moxie said to me, "you and I can take that trip we were discussing."

I thought of 350 Wayward Way, and the large, empty room in the photograph with the door in the corner and the rectangles on the floor. Secrets, I thought. Hidden in plain sight. "Maybe later," I agreed.

Theodora frowned. "Whatever playdate you two had planned," she said, "it will have to wait. Come along, Snicket. We've got to go to 350 Wayward Way."

CHAPTER TWO

350 Wayward Way turned out to be in a particularly deserted part of town. Theodora steered her shaky roadster past Diceys Department Store and then onto a street full of dead buildings with boarded-up doors and broken windows. It was like a garden that someone had stopped watering. Those gardens always look slightly sinister. You never know what's hiding amongst all the wild and ragged weeds.

"You know what I like about neighborhoods

like this?" Theodora asked, as the brakes squeaked us to a halt. "There's plenty of parking."

"There's plenty of parking because nobody wants to come here," I said.

"Not sensible, Snicket," my chaperone said, with a shake of her helmet. "Not proper. *We* want to be here. There are questions that S. Theodora Markson needs to have answered."

"What does the *S* stand for?" I asked.

Theodora glared at me. "Smart," she said. "You're a smart boy, Snicket, but you need to apply yourself."

"I've never really understood what that means," I said.

"It means your predecessor never gave me such problems."

"You must miss having him as an apprentice."

"I do."

"Maybe you should send him a bunch of heart-shaped helium balloons just to let him know you're thinking about him."

"Don't laugh at me, Snicket. I am not a puppet show. We're very lucky to get such a prestigious client as the Department of Education. You'll have to adjust your attitude accordingly. For instance, we are not to reveal anything about this case, or who has hired us to solve it. I expect my apprentice not to say a word about the whole thing."

"What is the whole thing?"

"I told you, we shouldn't say a word about it."

"How can I say a word about something I don't know about?"

She did not answer but got out of the car and slammed the door unnecessarily hard. I did the same. "Prestigious" is a word which here means "important or having great influence," although the Department of Education didn't look prestigious as we approached the door. It was a tall, thin building, sagging against another tall, thin building to its right, and being sagged on by a tall, thin building to its left. The tall, thin buildings kept going, saggy and shabby, all the way down the block, like grass curved over in the wind. Just over the door was a cardboard sign reading DEPARTMENT OF EDUCATION that I wanted to remove, just so I could see the words ROE HOUSE that were probably carved into the stone beneath it.

Before we could get to the door, it opened and a man walked out, putting on his hat and taking out a cigarette. Theodora nodded to him as he held the door open, and he turned briefly to her and said something she had to ask him to repeat.

"Do you have any fire?" he repeated.

"We are in fact here to investigate a case of arson," Theodora said, "but that is a secret I am not to reveal."

The man frowned impatiently and pointed to his cigarette to show what he meant. The cigarette sat tucked in his mouth, hanging over his beard, unlit.

"Oh!" Theodora said. "No, I'm sorry, I don't have any matches."

The man turned his eyes to me and I shook my head. I did in fact have a box of matches in my pocket, but I don't think adults should be encouraged to smoke. He frowned again and started to walk away before turning around and asking me a question.

It is not a question anyone enjoys hearing, especially people my age. It is the question printed on the cover of this book.

"I'm in a special program," I said, as Theodora stepped inside the building.

"Are you indeed," the man said. It didn't sound like it was news to him, or perhaps he just didn't care much. He reached up and took the cigarette out of his mouth and turned around and walked away. I watched him, but I didn't know why. He looked like nothing to watch. He was just a man, moving quickly down the block. At the corner he tossed his cigarette into a dented trash can with a noise louder than it should have been. Most of Stain'd-by-the-Sea's trash cans were as empty as its sidewalks. I stopped watching and followed Theodora in.

I'd expected to be in the large, empty room Moxie had shown me in the photograph. Instead I found myself in a small waiting area, separated from the large room by a wall that looked like it would fall over if you gave it one good push. In the middle of the wall was a swinging door, not swinging, and tacked to the door was a sign that said WELCOME TO THE DEPARTMENT OF EDU-CATION, WHERE LEARNING IS FUN! LEARNING IS IMPORTANT! said another sign, on another wall. There was one that said BOOKS ARE FOR LEARN-ING! that hung over a bookshelf, and one that said TAKE TIME FOR LEARNING! hanging over a table. On a table were a stack of stickers reading LEARNING! that you could affix to the bumper of your car or boat, and a bowl of badges read-ing LEARNING! that you could pin to your shirt or jacket or lampshade. They'd pinned a few of them to the lamp's lampshade, was how I knew, along with a small sign that read LEARNING! It seemed like a lot of learning.

There was a boy about my age going *clickety-clack* into a typewriter at a large wooden desk. His hair had been trimmed into a sort of tilted spike, like the fuse on a stick of dynamite, and his eyes were wide and not looking at us. When he was done typing the page, he took it out of the typewriter and put it on a large pile of other pages. Then he started up on another sheet of paper. He typed faster than I'd ever seen Moxie type, much faster. His hands hardly moved around the keyboard, as if he were typing the same thing over and over again. There had been a sign pasted onto the side of the desk, and the sign had probably said LEARNING!, but somebody had tried to unpeel it and now it was just a scratchy white mess, like a cloud you might stare at after a picnic. Through the flimsy wall I could hear more typewriters, plus the shuffle of papers and the other muttery noises of a busy office, but the boy behind the desk was the only person from the Department of Education to be seen.

"S. Theodora Markson," announced S. Theodora Markson, "and her associate. We have an appointment."

"Please wait," the boy said, without looking up from his typing.

Theodora sat in one chair and I sat in another, near the bookshelf. I took down a book that had been recommended to me by several people I didn't like.

The swinging door swung, and a tall, neatly dressed woman strode to the desk where the boy was typing and took a few papers from the tall pile. Pinned to her collar was a very shiny gold badge shaped like a lime, and pinned to her face was a smile that shone much less brightly. Theodora stood, but the woman did not look at us or say anything, just retreated back into the busy office. Theodora sat. I tried the book. A man gave his son Jody a pony, and Jody had to promise to take care of it. Then the pony got sick. I could see where this was going and put the book down. It was more pleasant to sit and think what the cloud looked like.

We waited awhile. The boy kept typing and typing and typing and then finally stopped but he was just scratching his elbow and then he was typing again. The tall woman made several trips through the swinging door and back again without looking at us. Theodora took up the book and seemed quite interested in it. I stood up. He might not talk to me, but I would talk to him, so I asked him if it would be much longer.

"I don't know," he said, and typed and typed and typed.

"You don't have to look busy on my account," I said.

Now he stopped. "I look busy because I *am* busy."

31

"So you say," I said.

"You don't have to take my word for it," the boy said, and pointed to the pile he was making. "Look at what I'm typing if you don't believe me."

"I'm not a math tutor," I said. "I don't feel the need to check your work."

"The Department of Education is a very busy office. We're in charge of every pedagogical institution in Stain'd-by-the-Sea. Read about us in the newspaper if you don't believe me."

"Why wouldn't I believe you?"

"All right then, Snicket."

I sat down and then stood up again. "You know my name, but I don't know yours. That doesn't seem fair."

"It's Kellar," the boy said. "Kellar Haines."

"Well, Kellar Haines," I said, "shouldn't you be in school?"

Kellar had been ready to start typing again, but now he blinked and looked down at his fingers. They were trembling a little bit. "Yes," he

said, and there was something about the way he said it, quiet and sad, that made me see the two of us a little differently.

The door swung open again, and the woman with the lime pin came out and looked at us at last. Then she looked at Kellar Haines. Then she looked behind her and then she smiled nervously and then she began to speak.

"Good morning" is what she said. "I'm Sharon Haines. I work here, which is the Department of Education. Yes, that is what it is."

"I'm S. Theodora Markson," said S. Theodora Markson, "and never mind who this is."

"Lemony Snicket," I said.

"This is my son Kellar," Sharon said, "and never mind him, either."

Sharon gave a little nod to indicate Kellar, and Theodora gave a little nod in my direction. Then they both smiled, Theodora first and Sharon after a few seconds, like a mirror running late.

"Perhaps we should talk in your office," I said.

"Yes, of course," Sharon said, leading us to the swinging door, and then she gave a sort of gasp. "No, let's just sit here, shall we? The Department of Education is very busy today. *Very* busy. And my desk gives me some kind of medical condition. My tongue swells up if I sit there too long, and I end up talking like my mouth is full of baby mice."

She sat down between us, and I watched Theodora nodding seriously at Sharon the way one adult has nodded at the nonsense of another adult since the first adult walked on the earth. "I think I have a medical condition, too," Theodora said. "Lately when I'm driving my roadster I have the peculiar sensation of everything being quieter than it should be."

"That could be because your helmet covers your ears," I said.

The two women looked at me the way you look at a leaky pen. I looked down at the floor. There was an ugly rug with ugly triangles on it in an ugly pattern. Underneath, I thought, were the rectangular marks I'd seen in the photograph. I wondered what was covering the floor in the office, on the other side of the flimsy wall. Desks, chairs. Whatever all those muttering people kept in their office.

"Perhaps I'd better tell you about the case," Sharon said, and she went to her son's desk and took something out of a drawer. It was a photograph, but we couldn't see it. It was facedown, and she left it that way in her lap when she sat back down. She sighed and looked behind her. Behind her was a wall. "There is a villain," she said, "who is putting every schoolchild in town in terrible danger."

I knew it, I thought.

Sharon gave us a long look. Kellar went type-type-type. "We have had some dealings with such a villain," I said. "It would probably be best not to say his name."

"It's Hangfire," Theodora explained.

Type-type-stop.

"Hangfire," Sharon repeated with a frown. "What do you know about him?"

"Not much," Theodora said. "He's violent and treacherous. You know the kind of man I mean."

"Yes, I do," Sharon said, with a nervous smile. Kellar started typing again. "I had a boyfriend like that in eighth grade."

"Me too!" Theodora was using a tone of voice I hadn't heard from her before. I regret to say that I'd have to describe it as a squeal. "He was always saying impolite things about my hair."

"Well," Sharon said, "I think it looks nice."

"Well," Theodora said, "I think *you're* nice."

"Nevertheless," I said, spoiling the party, "we're here to talk about Hangfire."

Sharon sighed again and rattled her fingers on the photograph. "Recently a local business was burned to the ground," she said. "Birnbaum's Sheep Barn caught fire in the middle of the night, and there was scarcely enough time to evacuate the sheep. The fire was not an accident. It was a crime."

Theodora turned to me. "She means arson," she explained, unnecessarily. You could not become an apprentice without knowing what arson is. You could not even start to study for an apprenticeship without knowing "arson." I even knew the original Latin term from which the word "arson" was derived.

"We'll assign this case extra-crucial status," Theodora said to Sharon, using an expression that meant absolutely nothing.

"I appreciate that," Sharon said. "As luck would have it, there was a witness to the fire, and I'm hoping you and your apprentice will go interview this man and see if he can tell you anything."

"A witness!" Theodora cried. *"Aha!"*

"For instance," Sharon continued, "he might say the arsonist had an unusual jacket, so it would help you find him and capture him."

"Unusual jacket! *Aha!*"

Theodora looked at me triumphantly, but I saw nothing triumphant about an imaginary jacket mentioned by a witness we hadn't met yet.

"Who is this witness?" I asked.

Sharon's eyes widened and she moved her hands up and down, over and over, like she couldn't decide whether or not to remove her ears. She looked over at her son and then down at her collar, and then she cleared her throat and answered my question at last. "Harold Limetta is his name."

"Harold Limetta?"

"Yes, Harold Limetta. I believe his name is Italian, although he lives here in town at 421 Ballpoint Avenue, walking distance from the library."

"We'll take my car," Theodora said. "Thank you for meeting with us, Ms. Haines."

"Call me Sharon," Sharon said, "and call me the minute you have an update."

"Of course I will," Theodora said. "After all, our progress is being evaluated."

Kellar stopped typing for a second and shared a look with his mother I didn't quite understand, but every family has a look they give each other that makes no sense to anybody else. "Yes," Sharon agreed, when the look was over. "Our progress *is* being evaluated. Do you have any more questions?"

"Yes," Theodora said. "How can I reach you outside of office hours?"

"I'll give you my number," Sharon promised. "I must say, I didn't expect so much kindness and understanding from such a prestigious investigator."

"It is you who are prestigious," Theodora said. "Come along, Snicket. We're done here. Let's head on over to Harold Limetta's house."

I was still staring at the photograph turned upside down on the desk. "I have a question," I said. "Why are schoolchildren in danger because a barn burned down?"

Sharon sat up in her chair and straightened

the creases on the coat she was wearing. I didn't like the coat and I didn't like its creases. "The Department of Education takes its mission very seriously," she said to me. "Even one schoolchild in danger is a terrible thing. Children are the future of the world, and we must keep them safe from harm. Every night I tremble thinking about how I'd feel if something terrible happened, even if it happened to somebody I did not know."

I made myself nod. I'd heard every word the woman had said, but I didn't mistake it for something that made sense. Her fingers slipped under the edge of the photograph, and she slowly began to turn it over. "If this jacketed villain burned down a barn," she said, "it stands to reason that he'd burn down a school." She leaned forward and looked very sternly at me. "I can guarantee you, young man, that it will probably happen. If you don't believe me, take a good, long look at this!"

With a flick of her wrist, like a magician at a birthday party, she turned the photograph over and I took a look. It was not a good, long look because there was nothing much to look at. It was a photograph of a barn, or at least it had been a barn, before it burned down. Now it was a great deal of ashes and a few lonely sticks of burned wood. The remains of a fire are not a nice thing to look at, but they are not a great danger to schoolchildren. I looked at the photograph and then I looked around the room I was in. There was no sign of the fishing industry. There was none of the necessary equipment described in *Caviar: Salty Jewel of the Tasty Sea*. Still, there was something fishy about the whole place. You might as well play along, I said to myself. Hangfire might be involved, and you might find Ellington Feint again and be able to keep your promise, and in any case Theodora is in charge, so you don't have much choice, do you, Snicket? No, Snicket, I don't. I looked at the photograph again, and then I looked at Sharon and thanked her for answering my question. We all stood up and said the usual things and Sharon led Theodora and me out of the Department of Education. I let the adults go out ahead of me and then stepped quickly back to Kellar's desk.

"You know that restaurant Hungry's?" I said. "You can find me there, when I'm not at the library or the Lost Arms."

Kellar looked up at me and spoke very, very carefully, as if he were walking through shattered glass. "I'll look up the address," he said, "just like you'll look up Harold Limetta."

"Your mother already told us Harold Limetta's address," I said, and then Sharon walked back in. Kellar went back to his typing and I went out. Theodora was already in the roadster, pushing her head into her helmet. I stood on the sidewalk for a moment, wondering about both of the people I had met inside. It was hard to figure them out, but that is true of almost everything when it is very hot outside.

"That went very well, Snicket," Theodora

said. "I'm glad Sharon gave me her phone number. I'm going to call her this evening and give her a full report."

"I think it's nice you're making friends your own age," I said.

Her smile faded and she started the motor. "You should have listened to what she said, Snicket. She said our progress is being evaluated."

"You're the one who said that."

"Well, Sharon agreed with me, and it's true. If you were a better apprentice, you'd remember I told you that someone from our organization was keeping an eye on us."

I remembered. Theodora was quite nervous about this person, whoever it was. I didn't think it was likely that it was Sharon Haines of the Department of Education. I had my own ideas. "I did listen to what she said," I said. "She thinks all of Stain'd-by-the-Sea's schoolchildren are in danger because someone burned down a sheep barn. That doesn't make much sense to me."

"Well, I'm sure Harold Limetta will be able to tell us more."

I looked down the empty block. The man who had asked for matches was long gone, of course. The dented trash can sulked on the corner. "Why would the Department of Education know about a witness to a fire?"

"It wasn't just a fire, Snicket. It was arson. Any apprentice of S. Theodora Markson should know what that means."

"What does the *S* stand for?"

She opened the passenger door. "Slide in, Snicket."

I slid in and squinted out the window of the roadster. The sun told me that it was about noon. It also told me that it was going to continue to beat down on Stain'd-by-the-Sea and make it blazing hot and that there was no point in arguing with it, because it was the sun and I was a boy of about thirteen. The sun was right. There was no point in arguing. The roadster puttered us through Stain'd-by-the-Sea, and I didn't say anything more to Theodora. She called herself an intrepid personage and said that was an expression which there meant an excellent investigator, and I didn't correct her. She called me ungrateful and I didn't disagree. I just sat in the heat and wished for an ice cream cone. Nobody brought me one. Maybe Harold Limetta has a freezer full of the stuff, I told myself. Peppermint ice cream in particular would really hit the spot.

But there was no freezer at 421 Ballpoint Avenue. I could tell that in a minute, when Theodora brought her automobile to a stop. A freezer is almost always made of metal, so when a house has been burned to the ground it usually remains there in the ashes, along with the oven, the wall safe, and any anvils lying around, each item a blackened gravestone for the home that has been destroyed. At 421 Ballpoint Avenue I could see a metal bench, which looked like it might have been by the front door, for taking off your boots. I could see a large set of small metal rectangles, each one about the size of a book, stacked up in several rows and surrounded by broken glass. I could see a metal picture frame, which might have held photographs of the Limetta children or grandchildren. But the rest of the house was nothing but ashes and smoke—thick gray smoke that was rising into the sky. I didn't know if it would block the sun and make it cooler. I didn't know whose pictures had been in the frames. I didn't know what it meant that Harold Limetta's house had burned down, just when we'd been sent to it. Fires were of grave importance to the organization of which I was a part. It would be a black mark on my record, I knew, to have suspicious fires occur and go unsolved and unpunished right under my eyes. Hangfire, I thought, I will find you and stop you. But I didn't know how to find him. I didn't know how to stop him.

I didn't even know for certain that this fire was his handiwork.

Ardere is the Latin, I thought. That's what they said in ancient Rome when they were talking about fire. But that was all I knew as I stood and waited for the smoke to clear.

CHAPTER THREE

When the smoke cleared, there was something to see in the rubble of 421 Ballpoint Avenue, but it was the Officers Mitchum. I preferred smoke. Harvey and Mimi Mitchum were the only police officers in Stain'd-by-the-Sea, but they spent less time enforcing the law and more time bickering over just about anything that struck their fancy.

"And let *me* tell *you*," Harvey Mitchum was saying to his wife, "that it was *Agnes* who had the idea, and *Harry* just played along, so by the time

Philip had him cornered the crime had already been committed."

"You're a half-wit," Mimi Mitchum said. "Carmen is the mastermind behind the crime, and if you can't figure that out for yourself you might as well toss your badge into the ashes."

"Carmen's no mastermind," Harvey said. "She's even more dimwitted than you are."

"How dare you call me dimwitted?"

"How dare you call me a half-wit?"

"It's crueler to say that wits are dim than that they're chopped in half!"

"Mimi, you're only proving yourself dimwitted when you say things like that."

"If I'm so dimwitted, how did I manage to solve the crime?"

One of the first things I'd learned upon arriving in Stain'd-by-the-Sea was that the only way to get the Mitchums to stop arguing was to interrupt them. "Excuse me, Officers," I said, and the officers turned to look at me the way they always did. It is the way you look at a squeaky door when you are trying to be quiet.

"What are you doing here, lad?" Harvey Mitchum asked me.

"Did I hear you say you've managed to solve this crime?" I asked. It is always better to ask a question than to answer one.

"Harvey was just arguing with me about a movie we saw," Mimi said. Her eyes moved suspiciously through the smoke from me to Theodora and back again. "How is it you happen to be here?"

Theodora put a gloved hand on my shoulder. "My associate and I were going to talk to Harold Limetta, the owner of this house, as part of an investigation."

Harvey frowned and kicked at the ashes on the ground. "And who, precisely, has asked you to investigate?"

"I'd rather not say," Theodora said.

"Well, I'd rather not have you poking through the scene of a crime," Mimi said.

"And I'd rather not have that kid around here either," her husband added.

"I'd rather not have you call me a kid," I said.

"I'd rather not have my apprentice talk like that to the police," Theodora said.

"I'd rather not have to listen to you discipline a child," Harvey Mitchum said.

"I'd rather not listen to my husband boss people around," Mimi Mitchum said.

"Sorry," I said, "is it my turn? I have a long list of things I'd rather not do."

It is not pleasant to have a number of people glaring and sighing at you at the same time, even if you meant for them to do it. As I'd planned, once they were done glaring and sighing, the Mitchums forgot all about asking us why we were there or who had sent us, and so the four of us were soon picking through the wreckage together as if we had never argued at all.

In one of my favorite books, a sad young man stumbling around outside finds a tiny strange man with a sack of magic crystals that change his life. My hopes weren't that high, but I kept my eyes open. Almost anything would do. Any kind of clue would be better than what I had now. What I had now was bupkes, a word which here means "The Department of Education told us to go interview someone about a sheep barn burning down, only to find that the man's house had burned down." The metal bench was still there, and the metal picture frame with the photographs burned out of it. The metal rectangles were still there too, stacked up like the books you were planning on reading next. My shoes crunched on the shattered glass. They're tanks, I realized. Tanks for fish or small animals. They're tanks and they'd probably be clues, I thought, if you knew what the mystery was.

"What do you know about Harold Limetta?" I asked the Mitchums.

"Not a lot," Harvey Mitchum admitted. "He's new in town."

"He moved into this house only days ago," Mimi said. "All anybody knows about him is that he is a leper."

"He's sick?" I said.

"No," Harvey said. "He studies moths."

"Then he's a lepidopterist," I said. "A leper is someone with a terrible skin disease."

"Nobody likes a know-it-all," Mimi said.

"He called us and said his house was on fire," Harvey Mitchum said, "but when we arrived there was no sign of him, although it looks like his moths were burned to a crisp."

Mimi pointed to some tiny black specks near the shattered glass of the tanks. They might have been moths, once. And it might have been Harold Limetta on the phone. "We were going to ask for him at Birnbaum's Sheep Barn," she said. "The barn supplied wool for Mr. Limetta's moths to eat."

"Birnbaum's Sheep Barn has also burned down," Theodora said, sitting on the bench before immediately getting up again and brushing the ashes off the back of her pants. It took her a long time.

"What do you know about these fires?" Harvey Mitchum demanded. "It's still too early to make assumptions, but I'd say both of you have something to do with all this. Lately, whenever there's a crime in Stain'd-by-the-Sea, we seem to find you and your whippersnapper poking around."

"We're here as professionals," Theodora said stiffly, finishing up with her pants.

"We'll do anything we can to help you solve this case," said the whippersnapper.

"You can help by butting out," Mimi Mitchum said. "And the same goes for you about butting, Harvey."

Harvey gave his wife an exasperated frown. "Mimi, I'll remind you that I'm an officer of the law, just like you are."

"You're not just like I am," Mimi said. "I'm a

brave and capable law enforcement official, and you're a nincompoop!"

"If I'm such a nincompoop, why are *you* the one who forgot to put the milk back in the refrigerator, so it stayed on the counter all night?"

"Well, *you're* the one who left the window open, so mosquitoes swarmed our bedroom!"

"Well, *you're* the one who didn't hang up your towel after your bath, so it stayed wet and clammy!"

Imagining the Mitchums getting out of the shower in clammy towels with the windows open and the air smelling of warm milk was a new item on my list of things I would rather not do. "Excuse me, Officers," I said, "my associate and I are leaving now. Please send my regards to Stewart."

Stewart Mitchum was the officers' son, and I did not really want to send him my regards. I could not think of anything I wanted to send him that would be accepted for delivery. "Stew's at school," Harvey Mitchum said. "He insisted that he stop working for us by making a siren noise out of the back of our car, and focus on getting a top-drawer education."

"How nice for him," I lied. A top-drawer education is a very high-quality one, but the highest-quality anything in the world wouldn't fix Stew.

"I'd suggest you do the same, Snicket," Mimi said, and gave me a stern look. "We'll be keeping an eye on you."

"And the milk," Harvey added, glaring at his wife. As a good-bye, I gave them a nod I had practiced for quite some time in the mirror. It was polite enough that no one could complain but not so polite that the person receiving the nod would think you liked them. I trudged through the ashes, trying to think. I had been taught to spend longer than a few minutes at the scene of an investigation, but I was not quite sure what it was that I was investigating. Start from the beginning, I told myself. The Department of Education was concerned about a suspicious fire, and pointed us toward a witness to the fire. Upon arriving at his home, we found it too was burned to the ground. There were moths, there were sheep. The Department of Education had a child working there and was convinced that schoolchildren were in danger. The whole thing was gibberish. Only a babbling buffoon would think it made any sense.

"This is starting to make sense," Theodora said, when we reached the roadster. "There's an arsonist who is putting the schoolchildren of Stain'd-by-the-Sea in danger. We've got to find him and stop him, unless it's a woman, in which case it is she who must be found and stopped."

"Two buildings have been burned," I agreed, "but why are schoolchildren in danger?"

"The Department of Education said they were in danger," Theodora said. "Do you think my friend Sharon is lying?"

"She wouldn't have to be lying to be wrong," I said.

"Don't simper nonsense at me, Snicket. I am not a baby. Our progress is being evaluated, and the case has been assigned extra-crucial status. We've got to speed up the investigation. I'm counting on your hard work and cooperation."

I took a last look at the ashes as Theodora started up the roadster. Hangfire, I thought. Is this your handiwork? No one answered.

"Snicket, don't be a Trappist monk. Answer my question."

"You didn't ask anything."

"Well, I meant to ask something."

"What is it?"

"It's *what are your suggestions?*"

"Let's go to Hungry's."

"Be sensible. You just want to have lunch with your friends."

"I work better on a full stomach."

"Well, two can play at that game, Snicket.

59

I'm going to go see Sharon Haines, and we'll see who comes closer to solving the case."

The roadster took us back through town. It was hot, and the sun kept glaring at me. It reminded me of Stewart Mitchum, who also liked to glare but was nowhere near as bright. Why would Stew tell his parents he wanted to focus on his education, I asked myself. And then I asked Theodora to drop me at the corner. If too many people see you getting rides everyplace, they get the impression you belong in a car seat. The corner was hot, too. Peppermint ice cream. Maybe Jake Hix will have some in his freezer for dessert.

From the outside Hungry's didn't look like anything special, and inside it didn't either. Certainly there wasn't anything special about the owner, Hungry Hix, a bitter woman with little patience for young people. What was special about the place was Jake Hix. He was a young man, but old enough to have a sweetheart and a job. The sweetheart was Cleo Knight, the brilliant chemist, and the job was cooking up the food at Hungry's. It is possible that his genius was more impressive than Cleo's, and in my case he gave away the food for free, as my funds were limited, a phrase which here means that Theodora didn't give me an allowance. When I walked into the room, he was standing at a blender that was whirring and crackling away at something the color of bricks. Watching him was Moxie Mallahan, sitting at the counter with her typewriter case hoisted up beside her. I almost didn't see who was sitting next to her until I was already inside. Nobody noticed me for a second—Moxie because she was watching Jake, Jake because he had his nose in a book, and Kellar Haines because he was pretending not to notice me as I sat at the counter with everybody else.

Jake looked up and turned the blender off. "How are you, Snicket?"

"Hot and starving," I said, nodding to Moxie.

"I have just the thing," he said, "but I'm going to make you taste it before I tell you what it is."

"Finally," I said, "a mystery I might solve. How's the book?"

Jake marked his place and tossed it to me. "Has anybody made you read this?"

"No," I said, looking it over. "I can never remember if that word in the title has one *A* or two."

"I have the same trouble," Moxie said sympathetically.

Jake cut big slices of homemade bread and tossed them into the oven to toast. Jake's bread was delicious. It took days to make and started with a small bowl of milk rotting on the windowsill. He should tell the Mitchums the recipe, I thought. They have some warm milk at their house. But Jake was telling me the book's story. "Two guys are friends, supposedly, and then one of them tricks the other one and he falls out of a tree and breaks his leg. The moral of the story seems to be, *some boys are mean at school.* I don't need a book to tell me that."

"If you want a good school story," I said, "try *The Children's Hour.*"

"I'm not sure I want a good school story," Jake said. He took the blender and poured the brick-colored liquid into three bowls. "I like a story that could never happen to me. If I want real life I'll read a newspaper."

"But the newspaper folded," Moxie said sadly.

At last Kellar Haines spoke up from his stool next to Moxie's. "But you don't go to school, do you, Jake? It sounds to me like a school story *is* something that could never happen to you."

Jake whisked the bread out of the oven and opened a jar of something orange. It looked like jam maybe. He spread it on the bread. "I can't go to school," Jake said. "My aunt counts on me to run this place."

Kellar looked around the diner and nodded. "What about you, typist?"

"I'm a journalist, not a typist," Moxie said firmly, handing him one of her cards. "My father counts on me, too."

"Doesn't anyone in this town go to school?"

"Lots of kids go to school in this town," Jake said.

"I hope so," Kellar said, running a hand through the spike in his hair. "Where would we be without a top-drawer education? Where would all the children be?" He turned to me and met my eyes. My eyes met him back, but I still felt there was something I wasn't seeing clearly. "And you, Snicket?" he said. "You're in a special program, if I'm not mistaken. That's why you were hired to investigate."

"You're not mistaken," I said.

"How's your investigation going?"

"I'm stopping for lunch."

"I don't blame you," he said. "The food's delicious. You know what it needs, though? Lime.

Lime from an Italian tree. My mother speaks Italian and loves limes, so maybe that's what gave me the idea. Of course, there aren't any Italian lime trees, not in this town. None at all. Still, some people waste their afternoons chasing after an Italian lime. There's a word for that. Can you think of the word, Snicket?"

I knew how I looked when I looked at Kellar. I've seen how people look at me when they have no idea what I'm talking about. "Many words come to mind," I told him finally. "Confused. Perplexed. Puzzled."

"Those aren't Italian words," he said, and wiped his mouth and looked around at all of us. Then he slid off the stool and left the place. We all looked after him.

"Odd kid," Moxie said, opening her typewriter. "Do you know him, Snicket?"

"His name is Kellar Haines," I said. "All I know about him is that he's a fast typist."

Moxie raised her eyebrows so high they almost disappeared into her hat. "Faster than I am?"

"I wonder what he was doing here," I said, instead of disappointing her.

"He came in about an hour ago," Jake said. "I made him a Reuben with extra Russian dressing, and he talked my ear off asking about you. He'd looked for you at the library and at the Lost Arms, so he could deliver a message."

"But he didn't deliver a message," I said. "You saw him walk right out the door."

We all looked at the door. It had a small square window toward the top, made from that kind of glass that you can't quite see through. You couldn't see the street or anything that was happening, just a few vague shapes. My whole day had been like that.

"Look," Moxie said. "He left my business card behind."

"I guess he thinks he doesn't need it," Jake said.

"Or," I said, "he doesn't want it to be found in his possession."

Moxie gave me a curious look and typed a few lines while Jake put the toasted bread in a pile on a plate and served up lunch.

"Here," he said, "eat up and tell me what you think."

It was soup, ice cold, a shock and a delight on such a hot day. The taste was sweet and crunchy and smooth and satisfying. Then I took a bite of the bread and something in the jam made me feel sparks on my tongue. It was a lunch of adventure. I felt my mouth grinning around the spoon.

"What do you think, Snicket?" Jake asked. "Does that cut the mustard?"

What he meant was, "Is this a successful soup?" and I told him it certainly was. "I don't taste mustard," I said, "but I do taste tomato and spring onion."

"And lime," Moxie said.

"But not from an Italian tree," Jake said with a smile.

I tasted again. "Maybe a little black pepper?"

"You're not getting the secret ingredient."

"Give us a hint," Moxie said.

Jake thought for a second. "Two hydrogen atoms and one oxygen atom."

"That's water," I said.

Moxie tasted again and smiled. "Watermelon."

Jake nodded. "Tomato-watermelon gazpacho. It's what they serve in Spain when it gets too hot. And the stuff on the bread is a habanero pepper jam I made myself."

"I wish all mysteries were that easy," I said.

"And this delicious," Moxie said.

Jake told us thank you and we kept eating. The food made me feel better. Good food always does. For a few minutes I stopped worrying about Hangfire and schoolchildren and arson and the Department of Education. I wasn't even worrying about Ellington Feint. I was just enjoying lunch, and my only worry was who was going to get the last piece of toast.

I should have kept worrying, though, because when I stopped worrying about the case, somebody else solved it. They solved it incorrectly and dimwittedly and disastrously, which is to say they didn't solve it at all. But solving a mystery is like naming a dog. If enough people call it one thing, that's the name that tends to stick. I was savoring my last sip of soup when Hungry's door swung open and the wrong solution to the mystery hurried in. It was S. Theodora Markson and she had a huge grin on her face, which was never good news. Sharon Haines was right behind her with a grin just as wide, and when Theodora waved to me, I saw that both women had matching freshly painted nails. The nails were wrong too. They were bright, bright yellow, brighter than anybody likes.

"There you are!" Theodora sang out to me, in a voice as bright as the fingernails. I'd never heard her use that voice, and I didn't like it.

"Tell him the good news," Sharon said, in a matching voice.

"We have good news, Snicket," Theodora said. "We've solved the case."

CHAPTER FOUR

"This calls for a celebration, if I do say so myself," Theodora said, grinning wildly at all of us. "The mystery might have been too difficult for a small child, but for an adult it was a snap." We all had to wait until she managed to finish snapping. You should only snap your fingers if you do it well. It's the same with surgery, or driving a forklift.

Sharon adjusted her shiny pin. "Don't take this personally," she said, "but if your associate went to a top-drawer school, he might have been smart enough to solve it himself."

"I doubt it," Theodora said. "He's been my apprentice for quite some time and shown no more promise than a bucket of juice."

"Speaking of beverages," Sharon said, "let's have one to celebrate. I always treat myself to a limeade when I accomplish something super-duper. The Italians call it *limeade*."

"Well, I call it a lovely idea," Theodora said, and turned to Jake. "Little boy," she said grandly, calling him something nobody ever wants to be called, even if they are a little boy, "limeade for my friend, and I'd like a glass of buttermilk." Then she removed her helmet, and Moxie and Jake blinked at her hair, which resembled yarn after a kitten fight, and then looked elsewhere so they wouldn't start laughing. Moxie looked down at her typewriter, and Jake got busy pouring drinks. If you've never had buttermilk and you're curious what it tastes like, good for you and don't be. "Sharon and I had our nails done, just us girls," my chaperone said, "and we put the whole thing together. Birnbaum's Sheep Barn provided wool for Harold Limetta's moths, so when the barn burned down, the moths were starving."

"I thought moths only ate wool in the larval stage," Moxie said.

"You're just a larva yourself," Theodora said, "so stop interrupting me. Whoever wanted to starve the moths didn't stop there. They lit Mr. Limetta's house on fire and the moths perished. Don't you see? The fires are a plot by someone who hates moths."

"You think that someone burned down two buildings," I said, "in order to kill an animal you can get rid of with a flick of the wrist?"

Theodora and her hair both nodded. "Ingenious, isn't it?"

"Ingenious" is a word which means "very, very clever." It is not the word I was thinking of.

"The arsonist is a moth-hater, all right," Sharon said, sipping limeade, "and my new best friend Theodora was telling me that she knew just who it was."

"We saw him this morning," Theodora said, "swatting moths as usual."

"You can't be serious," I said. "Dashiell Qwerty is a fine librarian."

"I'm as shocked as you are, Snicket," Theodora said. "In our line of work we've learned to trust, honor, and flatter librarians. But Qwerty is clearly a bad apple in a bowl of cherries."

"Dashiell Qwerty wouldn't hurt a fly," Moxie said.

"You're not listening, girlie," Sharon said. "He's hurting *moths*. The press always gets everything wrong."

"How did you know she was a member of the press?" I said.

"That's the wrong question," Theodora said.

"Be sensible, Snicket. What do you think we should do next?"

"Find Harold Limetta and talk to him," I said.

"No," Theodora said.

"Return to the scene of the crime and see if there's anything to indicate Qwerty was there," I said.

"That's strike two," Theodora said. "Two more strikes and you're out."

"We don't have time to play games," Sharon said, and pointed one strict finger at me. The polish on her nails was a flashlight in my face. "Your boss has already taken the next step. We've called the police, and the librarian will be arrested as soon as the Officers Mitchum can find him."

"Have they tried looking in the library?" I couldn't help asking.

"He's not there," Sharon said. "He's a fugitive. If you went to school, you'd know that a fugitive is a criminal who is running and hiding."

"Qwerty might not be running or hiding," I said. "He just happens not to be at the library."

"And he just happens to hate moths," Theodora said.

I looked at the plate of toast with habanero jam that Jake had prepared for us. There was still one piece left, but none of us were hungry anymore. "This isn't right," I said.

"I quite agree," Theodora said sternly, and downed her buttermilk. "A competent apprentice would have figured this whole thing out without any help. That's why my gal pal Sharon and I are going to go celebrate the end of this case, and you're not invited. I'll see you back at headquarters."

Theodora was grinning at Sharon, and Sharon was grinning at her. My chaperone had drunk the buttermilk, but I was the one with the bad taste in my mouth. Theodora slapped her helmet back on her hair, and the two women gave me a bright yellow wave good-bye and they were gone. For a few minutes nobody spoke. Moxie typed furiously until a page was through, and Jake cleared our bowls and stacked them in the sink with a busy pile of dishes that were already there. Like most people, he didn't do the dishes until somebody nagged him about it. He scooted the last piece of toast into the trash, and Moxie rolled a fresh sheet of paper into her typewriter, and then they both looked at me.

"What's going on, Snicket?" Moxie said finally. "What's this case about?"

"You heard my chaperone," I said.

"That was a lot of malarkey," Jake said, shaking his head disgustedly. There are other words for "malarkey," but I don't like most of them. "I've been to that library hundreds of times. Dashiell Qwerty is no arsonist."

"Anyone can see that," Moxie said, and poised her fingers over the typewriter keys. "Why don't you tell us about the whole thing?"

"I'm not supposed to discuss the case," I said.

Jake put his hands on his hips. "I'm not supposed to give you free food either, Snicket."

"But I'm your friend," I reminded him.

"Friends tell each other what's going on," Moxie said.

I pointed at the bandage on her arm. "That's what happened the last time I told my friends what was going on."

Moxie looked deep into my eyes. "It's Hangfire, isn't it?" she said to me.

"Hangfire?" Jake said. He clenched his fists.

"I don't know if it's Hangfire," I said. "I don't know anything at all."

"Hangfire was behind Cleo's kidnapping," Jake reminded me. "If you think that ruffian could be up to something, she could be in danger again. Snicket, you've got to tell us the skinny."

I looked at Jake and then at Moxie. They're right, I said to myself. You've got to tell them the skinny, Snicket. And so I did. "The skinny" is a phrase which just means "the secret information," but there wasn't much information at all. I told them about the barn. I told them about Harold Limetta's house and running into the Mitchums. That was all I told them. It was everything except the small tanks that lay burned in the wreckage. Moxie typed it all up and then turned to me.

"What does it mean?" she asked. "Who burned down the barn and the house? When will they strike next? Why would anyone do such a thing? Where is Harold Limetta?"

"Those are all good questions," I said. "I can't answer any of them."

"I have a question too," Jake said. "What can we do to help?"

"Do either of you know anything about the Department of Education?" I said.

They looked at each other and shook their heads. "We don't go to school, remember?" Moxie said.

"I went to school before I started living with my aunt," Jake said. "But it was just the usual song and dance of teachers and homework and recess and gum stuck to the underside of the desks."

"Maybe there's something in the archives of *The Stain'd Lighthouse*," I said. "Moxie, you found something about the fishing industry. Maybe you can find something about the Department of Education."

"Fishing industry?" Jake said. "What does that have to do with anything?"

"I'm not sure," I said.

"Will you tell us, when you are sure?" Jake asked.

I looked at Moxie's bandaged arm again, and then at Jake, remembering how desperate he was when his sweetheart was kidnapped. "Are you certain you'll want to know?" I asked.

They both nodded.

"Then I'll tell you," I said, and I thanked them and told them I'd see them when I saw them and I went out the door. It was late afternoon but the sun wasn't taking any time off. I looked up and down the block and tried to think of where I might go. The library, I thought. There's work to be done, books to be read. But you can't go there under these circumstances. Think, Snicket. Where else feels like home in this fading, frightened town?

My feet knew before my head did. In ten minutes I was at the corner of Caravan and Parfait. Black Cat Coffee was always the same, every time I was there. It was still just one room, long and narrow like a train car. There was still an enormous counter where you could sit and think. There was still a player piano in the corner, tinkling music that was sad but not weepy. There were still three buttons—one marked *A* that opened the hatch in the ceiling and lowered the staircase so you could reach the attic, one marked *B* that fired up the machine that made fresh bread, and one marked *C* that controlled the shiny equipment that brewed coffee, dark and strong, that I never drank. But there was no button to make Ellington Feint appear. It was a rare day that I didn't go to Black Cat Coffee, just on the off chance she might be sitting at the counter. The place was usually empty, but whenever I saw someone at Ellington's favorite spot, with a cup of coffee steaming next to them, my heart raced to think it was her even as my eyes told me that it was someone else. This day was no different. It was like all the other days during my time in Stain'd-by-the-Sea, where every person had a secret, and beneath all the secrets was a great, slippery mystery, like a creature lurking in the depths of the sea.

"I've never seen you here," I said to the person at the counter, "particularly during branch hours."

Dashiell Qwerty gave me a small smile and finished his cup. "I like the coffee," he said, his voice even deeper than usual. "I don't know when I'll get the opportunity to have another cup."

"Then you know that they're looking for you," I said.

Qwerty nodded. "You don't spend your life hanging around books without learning a thing or two."

"I know you didn't burn those buildings down," I said.

"You know no such thing," Qwerty said, and turned his empty cup over so it domed over the saucer. "There are people in this town who believe I'm a criminal, and soon there will be many more. There might as well be a picture of me in the dictionary, inked under *A* for *arsonist*."

"Are you saying that being a criminal is a matter of opinion?" I asked.

Qwerty smiled, but it was sad around the edges. "No," he said. "It's a matter of handcuffs," and then the police arrived. It was quick. There was a bang of doors, and Harvey and Mimi Mitchum rushed through. It was true. They had handcuffs, and they were around Qwerty's wrists in seconds. He frowned like I'd seen him frown a thousand times in the library, when he was looking for a piece of information that turned out to be disappointing, even when it was right where he'd known it would be. The Mitchums made him do this and that and told him he ought to be ashamed. They said I ought to be ashamed too, and when I asked what for, they just frowned. They opened the doors to Black Cat Coffee and told Qwerty to get away from the counter and into the patrol car, and then they argued over whose turn it was to say that and whether or not officers of the law should worry over whose turn it is when they're in the middle of arresting a notorious criminal. Qwerty stood up and met my eyes. His were nervous and moving quickly. I don't know what mine were.

"One favor," he said.

"Name it," I told him.

He pointed to his cup of coffee, and for the first time I noticed a book on the counter, a thick one with library markings on the spine. "I was away from the library on a delivery," he said.

"I didn't know you delivered."

"This was a special case," Qwerty said. "A woman felt she could not come to the library, as it would be dangerous."

"Dangerous for whom?"

Qwerty glanced at the bickering Mitchums and shook his head. "I arranged to deliver the book to her here."

"Here?" I said. "How old is this woman, exactly?"

"A little older than you, I'd say."

"Or maybe just taller," I said. "With unusual eyebrows, maybe? In the shape of question marks?"

Now Qwerty couldn't even smile. "Be careful, Snicket."

"Worry about yourself, Qwerty. You're the one going to jail."

"You might be going somewhere worse," said

the librarian. "If there's a book you wanted to finish, I'd do it soon, if I were you."

"And if you were me," I said, "what book would that be?"

"It's not for me to say," he said, with another look at the Mitchums. "They say in every library there is a single book that can answer the question that burns like a fire in the mind. You must find that book, Snicket, and read it."

"But the fires are burning in town," I said. "Who's setting them?"

"That's the wrong question," Dashiell Qwerty replied, and I watched him go. It was not nice to see. It was not nice at all. Seeing a librarian in handcuffs is like seeing a fish gasping on a rolltop desk. I couldn't look at it long, so I looked at the book and turned it over to see the title.

It was not a surprise, and yet I didn't see it coming. I picked up the copy of *Caviar: Salty Jewel of the Tasty Sea* and walked outside. Qwerty was already scrunched into the backseat of the station wagon and the Mitchums were arguing over the keys. Their boy, Stew Mitchum, was leaning out an open window in the front seat. When he saw me he started to imitate the sound of a siren, his usual job when he accompanied his parents on police business. This time, the siren sounded a little different—more like the growl of a wild beast. I didn't like it.

"That's a beautiful noise," I told him, so he'd stop.

"You're just jealous," Stew sneered. "I have a valuable skill, and all you have is your books."

I couldn't help looking up and down the block. Of course Ellington Feint wasn't there. She would have seen the police car. "You're right," I said. "I'm jealous. Every night I weep into my pillow that I can't make a good siren sound."

"I'm learning to do a lot more than that," Stew said.

"Oh yes," I said, "I heard you were enrolled in a top-drawer school. How's that going, Stew?"

"Not bad," Stew said, "but it's going to get better."

"Thanks to the Inhumane Society, I bet."

Stew's eyes grew dark. "How did you know?"

"I just guessed," I admitted.

"Guess all you want, Snicket. The sun is setting on you." He pointed to the sky, orange and red, with dark clouds drifting across it. "The sun is setting on the whole town."

"We'll see about that," I said. "See you around, little boy."

"Don't call our precious little angel a little boy," Mimi said sternly, and started up the engine of the car. She looked at me. Harvey looked at me. Stew looked at me. In the back, Qwerty looked at me. I was looking somewhere else. The Mitchums' station wagon roared off down the street with its animal howl of a siren, but I was looking at the sunset.

It was wrong.

I'd seen the sun rise at Black Cat Coffee, and

now the sun was setting in the same place it usually rose. I kept looking. It took me a moment to recognize what it was. Then it rang a bell, just as the bell rang from the tower of the Wade Academy. It was the signal for the citizens of Stain'd-by-the-Sea to put on their masks. The town was full of masks, hung on pegs and sitting on shelves, waiting for the faces that needed them. Some people said the masks served as protection from water pressure, and others said they filtered the salt from the air, and some said the masks were just superstition, left over from the days of the Bombinating Beast. It wasn't clear. But it was clear to me what I saw as I gazed at the sky, red and orange and blazing with fire.

CHAPTER FIVE

Help has arrived is what I was supposed to say, but it wasn't true. The fire engulfing Stain'd Secondary School was too enormous for one person to extinguish, and I was the only person there. Through the small slits in my mask, I watched the edges of the seashell building turn orange and red and begin to crumble. I had seen buildings burn before, as part of my training and as part of my childhood. I had seen small homes and enormous mansions devoured by fire, and I had seen flames destroy factories and symphony halls and houses of worship. A school seems worse, I thought as the fire roared into the sky. Even when the school is empty, it's a terrible thing.

The flames threw out a strange, hot wind that blew small shadows against the streetlights and telephone poles before falling to the ground. At first they looked like moths, but each moth disappeared to dust before it hit the pavement. It was not until one fluttered against my cheek that I realized what they were. The sky was filled with them, delicate and fluttering in the hot wind. They were the burned remains of wood and paper and cloth, a black blizzard of odd, fragile ashes turning to dust wherever they landed.

I slipped my library book into my shirt to protect it. There was nothing else to do. I could not leave a fire unattended. I'd learned that on the very first day of my education, before I knew what epistemology meant, or how to make a

grappling hook, or the location of the bath-
rooms. I paced up and down the sidewalk until
I found the nearest fire hydrant. It was useless
without hoses, of course. I looked up and down
the street and waited for firefighters to arrive.
Even through the mask, the ashes worked their
way into my mouth and made me cough.

Over my own wheezy hacking I heard the
whinny of a complaining animal, and from
around a smoky corner came two horses that
were either gray or white and covered in ashes.
The horses were both masked, just like I was,
and they were hitched to a jalopy, which is a
word for an automobile that looks like it could
fall apart if you touched it or even looked at it
sternly. The horses pulled it right to where I was
standing and then stopped, and all the doors of
the jalopy opened. Two masked men got out and
pulled a long, snaky object after them. I didn't
get a good look at it because the masked driver
of the car grabbed me and threw me into the

passenger seat. The jalopy seesawed as I landed on the upholstery. The upholstery was itchy and smelled like a barn.

I sat up and looked out the window. The two men were unrolling the snaky object, which I was glad to see was a firehose, and were fastening it to the hydrant as quickly as they could. The driver of the car was pointing wildly to the school and shouting something to them. I could not hear over the collapse of Stain'd Secondary's largest building, loud and slow like a defeated balloon. The firefighters told the driver something. The driver looked like he wanted to hear it again. He heard it again and nodded and ran back to the car and got into the driver's seat just as the bell in the tower, muted and sad over the sound of the fire, signaled the all-clear.

The driver threw off his mask. It was Prosper Lost. The proprietor of the Lost Arms was wearing a long beige coat that was already half-covered in ashes. He was breathing quickly. So was I, even when I'd gotten my mask off. I listened to our breathing, quick with soot and fear.

"Mr. Snicket," he said, after some time. "I am very happy to see you alive and well."

"What are you doing here?" I asked. "How did you know what was happening?"

"The same way you did, I expect," Lost said. "I looked at the sky." His voice and his manner had no trace of the sneakiness he usually demonstrated around me. It had vanished into thin air. Now he just seemed like a worried man who was done pretending. "Stain'd Secondary is the only school in town, Mr. Snicket. I hope this blaze is not too much for our official fire department."

"Are those two gentlemen the town's only firefighters?" I asked.

Lost gave me a solemn nod.

I looked as carefully at him as I could, for as long as I dared.

"Is there a volunteer fire department?" I asked finally, taking an enormous risk.

Prosper Lost shook his head, making a cloud of black dust appear. "This town has no volunteer fire department. The Talkie Brothers are Stain'd-by-the-Sea's only hope. Do you know what those ashes are in the air, Mr. Snicket?"

I knew the answer but did not give it.

"Those are burned pages. All the books in the school library are gone forever." Prosper Lost stopped and covered his eyes with his blackened hands. "I was so worried," he told me. "My daughter attends that school. But there was nobody in the place. The children had all gone home before the fire began."

"I didn't know you had a daughter," I said. "I've never seen her around."

"Ornette lives with her uncles," Lost said, looking out the window. "I miss having her near me, but I wanted to keep her safe."

"Safe places are getting scarcer and scarcer in Stain'd-by-the-Sea."

"Her uncles do dangerous work," Lost said,

with a nod to the firemen, "but I think she's better off there than with me. It's hard to find an acceptable place for a young person in this town."

I looked at Prosper Lost. His hands were shaking as he slipped the key to the jalopy into its slot. From under the hood, the reins of the horses snapped to attention. "I wholeheartedly agree," I said, and the horses pulled us away from the blaze. I tried not to think about the person I wanted to keep safe, who was likely in a prison cell. She is safe there, I told myself. She is safer there than she would be in this burning town.

Lost drove me to the Lost Arms with my head full of fire. Every time I blinked I could see the photograph of the burned barn, and the ashen remains of Harold Limetta's house, and the terrible destruction of Stain'd Secondary. Terrible fires resemble terrible people. They are unpredictable. They are selfish. They are deadly and ruinous. And no matter where they are prowling, no matter what treachery they are cooking up, they have something in common. They can be stopped. Not always, I thought to myself, and felt the library book in my shirt. Sometimes they just happen, Snicket, and there is nothing you can do. I didn't believe myself. My job as an apprentice was to investigate and stop villainy in this town. I had investigated the theft of a statue, and the Bombinating Beast was still hidden somewhere. I had promised Ellington Feint I'd help her rescue her father, but Armstrong Feint only seemed to sink deeper into the shadows of the Inhumane Society. I wanted to undo Hangfire's villainy, but with each passing day the fading town grew more and more desperate. There is nothing you can do, I agreed, as the horses pulled the jalopy through streets with ashes gathered on the ground like nightmare snow. There is nothing you can do, and everything you have done has made things worse.

We were there. Prosper let me out. I think I thanked him. My thoughts were so loud and fierce in my head that I cannot be sure. They were so loud and fierce that I didn't hear what was going on in the Far East Suite until I let myself in.

There was a party going on. Sharon Haines and S. Theodora Markson were standing in the middle of the room, directly under the light fixture shaped like a broken star, each with one foot in the air. They had blue, glittery hats on their heads that had the word HOORAY! spelled on them in very perky letters, and there were matching banners taped to the walls and over the window. It made the room look like it couldn't possibly have any troubles in it. The two friends were holding, in their yellow-nailed hands, shimmering glasses of a liquid so green it made me squint. The drinks made their nails look worse and vice versa. It was probably something lime-flavored, I thought, staring at Sharon's pin. The adults were staring at me, of course. A child who interrupts a grown-up party is always stared at. For a moment the only sound was some desperately happy music from an old-fashioned phonograph someone had put on my bed. I recognized the phonograph but not the music, which was a little too loud and a lot too perky. The women had probably been dancing. I did not want to think about what Theodora looked like when she was dancing. You shouldn't either.

"You're filthy," Theodora said, when they were done staring. "Wash that dirt off you before you come in here."

"It's not dirt," I said. "It's ashes."

"We heard about the school," Sharon said, with a solemn nod. "I'm very upset about it."

This was surprising, given her hat. "Nobody was hurt," I said.

"That's what we're celebrating," Sharon said quickly. "Theodora has solved a difficult and troublesome case, and we can put all this unpleasantness behind us."

"You were worried about schoolchildren in

danger," I said. "It doesn't seem to me that the case is over."

"Don't take this personally," Sharon said, "but you're almost as dopey as you are wrong. Not a single schoolchild is in danger. With the destruction of Stain'd Secondary, they have all been transferred to the Wade Academy, just outside of town. Normally, they only admit the best kind of students—the children of dukes, earls, counts, that sort of thing. You get the idea."

I got the idea.

"But because of the fire," Sharon continued, "the school has agreed to become the emergency replacement for each and every schoolchild in Stain'd-by-the-Sea. Thanks to the arsonist, they're all about to get a top-drawer education."

"And the arsonist is off to jail!" Theodora added. "The Mitchums have locked up Dashiell Qwerty, and he'll soon be taken by train to the city for the trial. This is a very important case, Snicket, and I deserve to celebrate its conclusion.

Sharon very considerately brought music and beverages, but you're not invited. The party's just for us girls."

She put her foot down and walked to the table to pour herself more of the green drink from a half-full pitcher she usually used to make her morning tea. "We need to investigate further," I said. "Dashiell Qwerty is not the arsonist. The Mitchums were just arresting him when the fire broke out at the school."

"The case is closed," Theodora said, but she would not look me in the eye.

I walked toward her so she could hear my whisper. "Our progress is being evaluated."

"It's being evaluated by my new friend," Theodora hissed, with a gesture toward Sharon. I looked over at her. She was beginning to sway to the music. It seemed unlikely that Sharon was the one from our organization who was keeping an eye on us. But it could be anyone, I reminded myself. Anyone but Prosper Lost, who thought the town had no volunteer fire department. "This case has gone splendidly for me, Snicket. It's you who are looking slatternly. Why don't you take a shower while Sharon and I hit the town? If you clean yourself up, and clean up this sty, maybe you'll end up looking as good as I do."

"Things are very wrong," I said. "Something terrible is happening right under our noses and we've got to find out what it is."

"It's rude to have secrets," Sharon called over to us. "Why don't you leave us alone, little boy, so the grown-ups can have their grown-up time? Go on, trot!"

I trotted, across the Far East Suite to the bathroom. I could not help slamming the door. "Slatternly" is a word which means "untidy and unprofessional." It is one of the worst adjectives to have on your evaluation as an apprentice. I sat on the edge of the bathtub and looked at my shoes. They were black with ashes. That was untidy. And I had spoken the name of our organization out loud. That was unprofessional. I was as slatternly as could be. I unbuttoned my shirt and found the book, *Caviar: Salty Jewel of the Tasty Sea*. Behind the door someone turned the music louder, and I thought of the old-fashioned phonograph. Keep trotting, I told myself. Take a shower.

When I was done, I stepped out of the shower but left the water on for a few minutes, to chase the last of the ashes down the drain. It was quiet. I opened the door a crack and took a peek. Sharon and Theodora were gone. They were probably hitting the town. I hoped it was hitting them back. I put on some pajamas and walked into the room. It was empty and it was a mess. I could hear what my sister would say about it, if she were in the room.

"It is a mess, L. But it's not your mess. Go to bed and forget about it."

"Theodora told me to clean it up."

"She also told you the case was closed."

"It doesn't matter," I said, and went to pour the green liquid down the sink. "I can't sleep in a messy room."

I could almost see her sitting on my bed, swinging her legs and smiling at me. I looked at her ankle and then at my own, and her smile got bigger. "That's why you never get enough sleep, baby brother. You stay up late trying to fix the messes of the world."

"If I don't fix things," I asked, "who will? Look out the window, Kit. This town has been showered in ashes because I haven't done my job. And it will likely only get worse."

"Imagining the worst doesn't keep it from happening," she said, as I took the phonograph off my bed and put it on the floor, out of my way. "The treachery of the world will continue no matter how much you worry about it, L. Get some rest, and let people take care of their own messes tonight."

"I didn't help you," I said, "and now you're going to prison."

She didn't say anything. One of the banners slid down the wall.

"I don't like talking to you like this," I said. "It's like you're a ghost."

"Look around," she said, with a gesture around the Far East Suite. "Look at everything in plain sight. The bed, the table, every object you see has likely been in the world longer than us, and they'll still be in the world when we're gone. It is the things that have a history, L. Compared to them we *are* ghosts."

She smiled at me, and then like a ghost she vanished, just as I was smiling back. She had never been there, of course, but it made me feel better to talk to her, even though I did not like it when she called me L. Now she was gone. I felt sad, but not as sad as I'd feel if I were a schoolchild about to be transferred to the Wade Academy with all the children of dukes and earls and counts. I cleaned up the room. You're not sad, I kept telling myself, but it felt only the tiniest bit true. I wasn't sad the way a spider isn't an insect.

There was still glitter on the floor when I was done. I went to bed, sliding into the covers as if into an envelope. I looked up at the painting that hung above my bed as usual, a little girl holding a dog with a bandaged paw. Who would paint such a thing, I wondered. First he painted the little girl and nobody cared, so he added a dog. Still nobody cared, so he added a bandage on the dog's paw, and now it's hanging in the Far East Suite watching me try to sleep. How long has that dog been hurt? How long has the girl been watching?

Look at everything in plain sight. The bed, the table, every object you see has likely been in the world longer than us, and they'll still be in the world when we're gone. It is the things that have a history, L.

People often forget to look at something right in front of them.

I sat up in bed and quickly turned the light on. I knelt beside the old-fashioned phonograph and looked carefully at it. It could be anybody's, I told myself. It looks like Ellington Feint's, but that doesn't mean it is. I picked it up and turned it over and then saw a word, just one word stamped into the machine, right where the arm with the needle lay waiting to make the music play.

It was the wrong word. It made me take three steps back.

I hurried to the bathroom and splashed cold water onto my face. The book was sitting on the edge of the sink, *Caviar: Salty Jewel of the Tasty Sea*. It was heavy in my hands. Don't smash the phonograph, I told myself. Don't kill the messenger just because he brought bad news. "Kill the messenger" is a very old phrase. You can find it in the works of Sophocles, an ancient Greek who wrote more than one hundred plays. Only seven survived. The other ninety-something plays could be about eating lobster in synagogues, for all anyone knew. I was thinking anything I could, anything at all, to stop myself from thinking what I was thinking. I was taking the word I had seen, the wrong word on the phonograph, and using it to fill in a blank, as in a crossword puzzle. It made the puzzle ugly and unspeakable. "Unspeakable" means you should not speak about it, and sure enough no one came around to speak to me about it. S. Theodora Markson did not return from hitting the town. Ellington Feint did not show up for her library book. Even my sister didn't appear, not even in my head, to speak with me about it. I was the only one. I spoke myself to sleep, speaking about an unspeakable thing, in an empty room.

CHAPTER SIX

In the morning Jake Hix was at Hungry's fixing
a Hangtown fry. It is the perfect breakfast after
a rough night. Everyone in the place needed one.

"We were wondering when you'd turn up,"
Jake said, grabbing oysters out of a bucket of ice.
I sat at the counter next to Cleo Knight, who
looked exhausted and cranky. So did Jake. So did
Moxie, who had her typewriter out. So did the
men sitting on the other side of Moxie. I'd seen
them once before, but this was my first good

look at them. They both had bandages on both their hands, and they both had wrinkled and blackened uniforms reading OFD, but other than that there was nothing alike about them. They were of different sizes, shapes, nationalities, facial expressions, hair lengths, ear sizes, nose shapes, mouth curves, brow furrows, and wrist-watches. Hungry Hix, who was wiping down a booth, also looked exhausted and cranky, but she always looked exhausted and cranky. If you were Hungry Hix, you'd look exhausted and cranky too, just from being Hungry Hix.

"I had a lot to think about," I said to Jake, and said hello to Cleo and Moxie. My chaperone still hadn't come back by morning, so I'd treasured my time alone in the Far East Suite, thinking.

"I'm sure you did," Cleo said. "Not long after Jake told me you were investigating suspicious fires, a suspicious fire started. We rushed to the scene to see if we could help."

Moxie was typing so furiously she couldn't

look up. "Snicket," she said, "these are the Talkie Brothers, our town's only firefighters."

They raised their bandaged hands to me in a salute, which I tried to copy. The Talkie Brothers didn't seem to be very talky. They didn't seem to be brothers, either.

"I also think the fire's suspicious," I said to my friends.

"So you know already," Jake said. "I figured as much." He opened a drawer and took out a large rubber glove and a small, curved knife. While he talked to me he held each oyster in a gloved hand and expertly shucked it. The word "shucked" means to take the part you can eat out of the shell. It looked brutal and delicious. "The Dilemma got us there just in time," Jake said, referring to Cleo's very fast and very beautiful automobile. "Something went wrong when they turned on the hoses. Instead of putting out the fire, the water only made it worse. Cleo and I had to pull the Talkie Brothers out of the blaze."

Cleo nodded solemnly. "I know what went wrong," she said. "It was sabotage."

"That's a strong word," I said. Jake was done with the oysters and rolled the edible parts around in some bread crumbs before tossing them into a pan where bacon was already sizzling.

"It refers to a person damaging or destroying something on purpose," Moxie said.

"I know what it means," I said. "For complicated reasons, I had to learn that word in kindergarten. Why do you think the hoses were sabotaged?"

Cleo shook her head. "Not the hoses," she said. "The hydrants. It wasn't water the Talkies poured onto the fire. It was some chemical."

"Some chemical," I repeated, looking into Cleo's eyes. She blinked back at me. Cleo Knight was a brilliant chemist. A brilliant chemist would no more say "some chemical" than a brilliant librarian would say "something to read" or a brilliant musician would say "some music." The expected answer is "atropine" or "selections from *The Goncourt Journals*" or "*Contrasts for Violin, Clarinet, and Piano*." Not "some chemical." Very, very slowly, Cleo's eyes began to move. They moved in the direction of the only adults in the place—the Talkie Brothers and Hungry Hix, who was picking up a rag she had dropped. Drop it, I thought. Drop it about the chemical and ask something else.

"How about you, Moxie?" I asked Moxie. "Did you find out anything about the Department of Education?"

Moxie looked at me as Jake cracked some eggs into the pan. He watched over them like a wizard. He added a little cream from a pitcher and then something green and leafy from a little glass bowl. I was wild to devour it, but when Moxie shook her head, my stomach felt shivery instead. I nodded. We couldn't talk here. There was a short list of places in Stain'd-by-the-Sea where I could talk with my associates without fear, and the list kept getting shorter. Hangfire had cast a pall over the town—a phrase which here means "made things shadowy and quiet"— and now he had cast a pall over the room. Jake went and turned on a radio playing music that made me think of Ellington's phonograph. The pan sizzled away for a while, and then he divided up the Hangtown fry for everybody, on big plates with toasted bread and glasses of orange juice on the side and a few shakes from a bottle of spicy vinegar for those who liked it. I liked it. The whole thing was delicious. It was delicious, but I couldn't finish it. "Some chemical," I kept thinking, with each bite, and then I thought of something else I'd heard that didn't make sense. I pushed my plate away.

"No way, Fay Wray," Jake said, using one of his favorite expressions as he looked at my cluttered plate. "Don't do this to me. Do you know how hard it is to get fresh oysters in this town nowadays?"

"It's worth it," I said. "This is a great breakfast like *The Wind in the Willows* is a great book."

"Then why are you eating it like it's as lousy as *Old Yeller*?"

"I guess I need some fresh air," I said. "Anyone want to take a walk?"

"I do," Cleo said, and pushed aside her plate.

"So do I," Moxie said, and pushed aside hers.

The Talkie Brothers frowned at us. Watching Stain'd-by-the-Sea's only firefighters try to eat a Hangtown fry with their hands bandaged was not doing anything for my appetite. Jake wiped his hands on his apron. "Where are you thinking about walking, Snicket?"

"I thought I might go visit a prestigious client," I said.

"I think I'll go with you people," he said.

"You'll do no such thing," growled Hungry Hix from the far end of the room.

"All right," Jake said to his aunt. "But I do need to take the garbage out."

"Come right back when you're done," Hungry said.

"As soon as the garbage is in the proper receptacle, I'll be back behind this counter," Jake promised, and he hung up his apron and picked up a metal barrel full of eggshells and other trimmings. "There's no charge for breakfast, by the way," he said, although he'd never charged me for anything since I'd arrived in town. "Anyone who helps out in a town emergency gets a free meal."

"I suppose that's all right," Hungry said, with a scowl. The Talkie Brothers nodded their thanks and Moxie clicked her typewriter closed and we walked out of the diner onto the sidewalk. It was still morning and it was still very hot, but the air was coiled up like it was holding its breath. It felt like another disaster was coming, or maybe it was just rain.

"It really was a good breakfast," I told Jake, as we stepped outside. "It was much, much better than *Old Yeller*. I'm sorry I wasn't a member of the clean-plate club."

"That always sounded like a boring club to me," Jake said, hoisting the garbage pail onto his shoulders. "Let's take the Dilemma. Cleo shouldn't be seen much in town anyway."

"You worry too much about me," Cleo said.

"If I don't worry," Jake asked, "who will?"

"You can't go with us," Moxie reminded him. "You promised your aunt you'd be right back."

"I said I'd be back as soon as this garbage was in the proper receptacle," Jake said with a grin. "That might take some time."

We joined Jake in a grin and headed down the block to Cleo's car. She opened the back and Jake put the garbage pail in the trunk, which was not the proper receptacle, while I gazed at the shiny automobile. It was a marvel of a machine. I can say without a doubt that riding in that vehicle was one of the highlights of my time in Stain'd-by-the-Sea. The Dilemma went down the street like it could fly if it wanted to but it didn't want to show off. I sat and gave directions and listened to the humming engine as Cleo nimbly spun the wheel.

"Can we talk now?" I said.

"We probably could have talked in the diner," Jake said. "My aunt's a grump, but she's not a villain, and the Talkie Brothers are firefighters. If you can't trust firefighters, who can you trust?"

"I don't know anymore," Cleo said sadly. "Something's happening in this town. The people inside this Dilemma might be the only ones I trust anymore."

"What about the Bellerophon brothers?" Moxie asked. She was talking about Bouvard and Pecuchet, better known as Pip and Squeak, two young men who had taxied us out of a number of tight spots.

"We can trust them," Jake said, "if they're still around. I haven't seen them for a little while."

I looked out at the lonely streets. "Maybe

their father isn't sick," I said, "so they don't have to drive his taxi."

Jake opened his mouth to say something and decided to say something else. "Tell Snicket about the chemical."

"It has a complicated name I won't bother you with," Cleo said, "but I recognized it when I smelled it at the scene of the fire. I've had that strong, briny scent in my laboratory for weeks and weeks. I'm working with it myself."

"It's part of the formula for invisible ink?" Moxie asked.

Cleo looked over at Moxie. "This is off the record," she said, "but yes, it is."

"Are you close to finishing the formula?"

Cleo shook her head. "Not as close as I'd like to be."

"You'll get there," Jake said, and patted her hand. "I know you will."

"Don't distract the driver, Hix," Cleo said, but she was smiling. I smiled too. It is good to see people happy with one another. It is a glimpse of a world in which everyone is that way. A happy world might be boring, I told myself, but watching Jake grin at Cleo grinning at Jake grinning at Cleo and back again, I thought it was worth the risk.

The Dilemma stopped at the corner, so smoothly it was as if we had never been moving. I got out and stood in front of the dented garbage can. Cleo frowned into it, and reached down to retrieve the cigarette the man had thrown away. No one throws away a cigarette that they haven't lit.

"What are we doing here?" Jake asked, looking first at his sweetheart and then at me.

"I thought Kellar Haines might be able to help us," I said, leading the way down the block.

"That guy?" Moxie said with a frown. "Everything he says is like a foreign language."

"I wish I'd taken Italian at my school," I said, "instead of Esperanto and Morse."

"I learned a few Italian cooking terms from Zada and Zora when I was small," Cleo said.

"You must miss them," I said, remembering the twin servants who had cared for her until they had to move away.

"I hope my work will eventually bring them back to town," Cleo said. "Then I might learn more than *anguilla Livornese* and *granita di nocino*."

"Do you know the Italian term for 'lime'?" I asked.

"*Limetta*," she said, but the answer had come to me along with the question.

"Limetta," Moxie said, "like the witness to that barn fire."

"There aren't any Italian lime trees around here," I said, "even though Sharon Haines speaks Italian and loves limes."

Moxie switched her typewriter case to her other hand so it wouldn't bump against my knee. "That's what Kellar said."

"There's no such person as Harold Limetta," I said, remembering the pin on Sharon's collar. "That's what Kellar was trying to tell us. His mother made up the name of a fake witness in order to trap a real librarian. Sharon Haines told us a story about Harold Limetta, and then stuck close to Theodora, making sure the case got solved the way she wanted it to be solved."

Cleo frowned. "But why would the Department of Education want to frame a librarian for arson?"

"That's the wrong question," Moxie said.

"Well, let's go find out what the right one is," I said, as we approached the row of thin, curved buildings.

"Snicket," Moxie said, "there's something I need to tell you."

"What's the news?"

"I looked through the archives of *The Stain'd Lighthouse*, but there wasn't a single article about the Department of Education."

"I can't say I'm surprised," Jake said. "That's not the sort of thing most people would be interested in reading about."

"That's not the reason," Moxie said. "Our newspaper wrote about boring things all the time."

We'd reached the door of 350 Wayward Way. We all frowned at the saggy building, except Cleo, who was frowning at the cigarette.

"Then what is the reason?" I asked Moxie.

"Stain'd Secondary is this town's only school," she said.

"You mean it *was* this town's only school," Cleo corrected, and put the cigarette in the pocket of her coat. "It's gone now."

"And the students have been transferred to the Wade Academy," I said, and walked into the building. The waiting area was waiting for us, with all of its LEARNING! and the book with the sick pony still boring on the table. The wall in front of me still looked flimsy, and there was still a half-unpeeled sticker looking like a curious cloud. Kellar was not at his desk, but I could hear the sounds of the busy office on the other side of the swinging door.

"Hello?" I called, but Moxie put her hand on my shoulder.

"Snicket," she said, "a Department of Education is in charge of every pedagogical institution within the town limits. But if there's only one school, then there's no Department of Education."

"No Department of Education?" Jake said. "Then where are we?"

I stretched out both arms in front of me, and gave the wall a good push. I was right. It fell down, quickly, with a gust of air that sent some typed papers rippling off Kellar's desk. I didn't watch them fall. I was staring at a room I had seen before, large and empty, with rectangular shapes on the floor and a door in the far corner. The only difference between the room and the photograph Moxie had shown me was a small machine I did not recognize at first, a box with two wheels spinning slowly, winding a long shiny strip around and around. It was an old-fashioned tape player, and when I flicked the red switch, the sounds of the office stopped.

Moxie walked to me, her footsteps echoing in the empty room. "Look at this," she said, and handed me one of the typed sheets the falling wall had sent fluttering. I looked.

Look busy. Look busy look busy, Look busy look busy look busy—look busy look busy—look busy, look busy look busy. "Look busy," look busy look busy. Look busy look busy? Look busy, look busy look busy.

"Look," busy. Look busy look busy look busy. Look busy look busy, look busy look busy look busy. Look busy look busy? Look, busy, look, busy;

```
look busy look busy (look busy, look
busy) look busy look busy look busy.
```

The words were typed over and over again, in tight, neat lines. I'd told Kellar he didn't have to look busy. Kellar'd told me he was looking busy because he was busy. He'd practically dared me to look at what he was typing. Cleo and Jake peered at the page over my shoulder.

"What is all this?" Jake asked me.

"It's the rest of Kellar's message," I said. "He was trying to tell me everything. There's no Harold Limetta. There's no Department of Education. This whole case has been nothing but deception."

Cleo put a hand on my shoulder. "Snicket," she said, "tell your friends what's going on."

"Do you know why he calls himself Hang-fire?" I asked.

"Villains always choose spooky names," Jake said.

"It was weeks before I thought to look it up in the dictionary," I said. "It refers to something that takes a bit of time before it works. It usually describes explosions or blastings. But people use it in other circumstances, too. It can describe a slow-acting poison, or a tree that weakens for years before it falls. There's a brand of old-fashioned phonograph called Hangfire, because it has a mechanism that allows the needle to hover over the record until the exact moment you want the music to play."

There is a look people give you when they are interested but they do not know what you are talking about. Moxie opened up her typewriter and sat on the floor to take notes. "So?"

I pointed to the floor where the papers had lain, and my associates looked at the small rectangular marks that were there. "When this building was the Roe House," I said, "they used special tanks for the baby sturgeons. But the tanks were moved from 350 Wayward Way to the Colophon Clinic, and then moved again to 421 Ballpoint Avenue, to concoct the ridiculous story about hating moths. The treacherous needle was hovering all the time, waiting to play a song that framed Dashiell Qwerty for arson."

"But why would Hangfire do all that?" Cleo asked.

"That's the wrong question," I said sadly. "The right question is, what did they do with the rest of the equipment from Roe House?"

"You mean someone's making caviar someplace?" Moxie said.

"I don't think so," I said. "Caviar is made from the eggs of fish. The eggs I'm thinking of hatch into tadpoles with very sharp teeth."

Jake paced around the empty room. "I can't make head or tail of that speech," he said. "None of it makes sense. I thought we interrupted Hangfire's plans. We rescued Cleo and shut down that horrible clinic."

"All those shackles," Cleo said, with a shudder, "ready to chain up hundreds of children."

"And now all the children in town are in one place," I said. "All of them but us."

Moxie looked up from the typewriter and frowned in thought. "Does 'truancy' mean what I think it means?" she asked.

"It refers to people who neglect their duties," I said, "but mostly it's used to describe children who don't show up at school. Why do you ask?"

She pointed at why she was asking. A beige van had pulled up to the curb, right ahead of Cleo's Dilemma. It looked harmless enough except for the writing on the side. It did not say FLOWERS or PACKAGES or anything you want to come in a van. It said DEPARTMENT OF TRUANCY, and the doors of the van were opening.

"I suppose in a town with one school," Jake said, "there's no more need for a Department of Truancy than a Department of Education."

"I suppose not," I said.

Two people got out of the van. One was a man and one was a woman, I thought, although it was difficult to be sure. Both of them were wearing long coats, wrong for the heat, and both of them were wearing masks. I had seen these masks many times, but they still unnerved me. "Unnerved" is a word which here means I didn't want to look at them. It didn't matter. The people wearing them were coming toward us, whether I wanted to look at them or not. One figure—the man, if it was a man—was holding something behind his back. I didn't want to see what it was. I was already scared quite enough.

"Why are they wearing masks?" Jake asked. "I didn't hear the bell ring."

"They're the ones who ring the bell," I said, and moved cautiously toward the far corner. The door, I thought. A back room, an exit someplace.

"How did they know where to find us?" Moxie asked, but they were already through the front door. For a moment we all faced each other. There are more of us, I told myself, than there are of them. But this is something all children say about all adults at one time or another, and it never seems to do any good.

"You children are truants," the woman said, instead of "hello." "We're here to take you to school."

"I don't go to school," Moxie said.

"None of us do," Cleo said.

"Children like yourselves shouldn't be messing around in abandoned buildings," the woman said. Her voice was muffled and buzzy behind her mask, or maybe she was trying to disguise it. She needn't have bothered. She wasn't wearing her shiny pin, but even as I moved toward the back of the room, I could see her bright yellow fingernails. "Get in the van and you'll learn the value of a top-drawer education."

"That's very sweet of you to say," Moxie said. She was using her good, polite voice, which she'd been taught was the journalist's best tool. It seemed unlikely to me that it was the right tool for the job. "We appreciate your interest in our ongoing development, but there's no need to bother yourself with troublesome underlings. We'll be on our way."

The man pointed through the door to the waiting van, and then brought his other hand from behind his back to reveal a large, carved club, a little longer and a little thicker than a baseball bat. It was made of black wood, and the carvings were at the very end of it. They were rough, angled carvings, as if the carver had been angry when he used his knife. Still, though, I could see what they depicted. I could see the face of the Bombinating Beast. I trembled backward a few more steps, but my associates stepped toward the front door.

"We can't get in that van," I told them.

The man walked swiftly toward me, swinging his weapon. Cudgel, I thought, would be another word for it. Staff. Wedge. I tried to remember what a billet was, exactly. I wished Dashiell Qwerty were there with a dictionary.

"If this man attacks me," I said, "with his club or cudgel or staff or wedge, you'll have time to escape."

"There's no need to show off with words," the masked woman said.

"It makes me feel better when I'm frightened," I said, and the man stepped closer. I could see his eyes blinking behind the slits in the mask, and when I reached my hand back I felt the knob of the back door. "Would 'billet' be appropriate?" I asked him. "I can't remember the exact definition of 'billet.'"

He didn't say anything. It wouldn't have mattered if he had.

"We can't let him hurt you," Moxie said.

I just looked at her bandaged arm. There are some things you cannot explain to anyone, even when they have been explained to you, over and over, almost since the day you were born.

"We're not going to hurt Mr. Snicket," the woman said calmly. "That's the deal we struck. But you other four children are coming with us."

"Four?" Cleo said, as Moxie and Jake looked around the room for a quick count.

The man reached behind me, and for a moment I felt his hand on mine as he turned the knob and the door heaved open. It felt like any other hand. Behind the door was just a small closet. It had a few buckets in it and a salty smell. It was damp, probably from a leak. And huddled on the ground was Kellar Haines. His wide eyes were frightened. All of him was frightened. The man reached down and hoisted him to his feet. Kellar met my eyes as he was dragged past me.

"I'm sorry," I told him. "I know you tried to warn us."

My associates watched in silence as the man brought Kellar to the front of the room. The woman put her hand on her son. The man looked back at me with the carved thing in his hand. You could just call it a stick, I thought.

"Don't get into that van," I said, and took a few steps in the adults' direction. The man gestured with his weapon, just slightly. Just slightly was enough.

"You act like we're doing some terrible thing," the woman said to me. "We're simply taking four young people to school."

"Then why are you wearing masks?" I asked.

The man hoisted the club in his hand and brought it smashing down onto Moxie's typewriter. Everything shook with the blow, and the journalist's device shattered across the room in a galaxy of pieces. Somebody shrieked in surprise—Jake, I think. The rest of us just stared at the savage, lost sight of the ruined typewriter that lay scattered like alphabetical bones. Then the woman opened the door, and Kellar, then Jake and Cleo, then Moxie with her eyes on the mechanical bits on the floor, and lastly the masked man walked out of the building. Moxie looked back at me.

"I don't understand," she said. "Why aren't they taking you?"

"I'm in a special program," I said, and followed them out. The air still felt like rain. The man ushered everyone into the van, but he still didn't say anything. His voice could have sounded like anything. He could imitate the voice of anyone, anyone at all. He might not have even had a real voice, not anymore. When Theodora and I had first arrived at the Department of Education, he'd asked us if we had any fire just to see if we recognized him. We hadn't. It was wrong not to recognize him. I was wrong to watch the van pull away from the curb. It drove down the street and turned a corner and my friends disappeared and it was all wrong, all of it exactly wrong.

CHAPTER SEVEN

S. Theodora Markson was on the floor of the Far East Suite, picking up glitter with her bare hands. She did not look up when I opened the door. I noticed that the yellow polish on her nails was almost gone. Here and there were little bits of it, but the rest of it had been scratched away. I felt the same way.

"Where have you been?" she asked me, still facing the ground.

"I might ask you the same question."

"I forbid you to talk to me that way," Theodora said, but she still wouldn't look at me. "I am the chaperone and you are the apprentice. I demand a complete account of your whereabouts since we last spoke."

I looked around the rest of the room. Things were missing. Theodora's suitcase was on her bed, closed up tight.

"I waited for you to come home all night," I said, "and slept a little bit, and then I got up and got dressed and went to breakfast."

"And then?"

"And then some friends of mine were abducted under the threat of violence and forced into a van." I knew better than to call them associates in front of Theodora, whose definition of "associate" was "someone who has completed our organization's formal training." My definition was more useful.

"Did you get the license number of the van?"

"I don't need the license number," I said. "I

know who was driving, and I know where it was going."

One of Theodora's hands opened, and I could see the glitter she'd piled up inside it. Nothing else moved. "What are you going to do now?" she asked finally.

"The abductors thought nobody would come after them," I said. "They were wrong. I'm going to rescue them."

"You can't," my chaperone said, on the floor. "The case has been solved, Snicket. I've packed up my things, and I expect you to do the same. We are leaving Stain'd-by-the-Sea on the next train."

"You're wrong," I said.

"I'm not wrong. I've packed my suitcase."

"You have enough wrong to fill fifty suit-cases and a garment bag," I said.

Theodora pounded her fist on the floor, and the glitter fluttered briefly and then fell back down, like a flock of pigeons when you walk through them. Then, finally, she raised her head to look at me. There was a bruise on her face, long and oddly shaped, running up from her cheek to curl near her eye. I knelt down quickly. If you have a bruise you do not want it touched, but everyone who cares about you will want to touch it, in the hope of somehow making it better.

"What did they do to you?" I asked.

"I think you can see for yourself," she said.

"They struck you."

"They struck a *deal*," she corrected. "We leave town and you don't have to go to that school."

"They're monsters," I said. "We'll go straight to the Mitchums and tell them what's going on."

She shook her head. It made her wince. Her hair looked like it might be wincing, too.

"We have a job to do," I said. "Something terrible is going on in this town, and we have to stop it."

"That's not our job," she said quietly. "We're not detectives and we're not lifesavers, Snicket."

"If we're not going to help people, why did we come here?"

"You can't help them. You're only an apprentice—and a child."

"But you're more than that."

Theodora shook her head and crawled over to sit on the bed, next to her suitcase. "I'm not like you," she said, with a great, shuddering sigh. "I'm not smart, Snicket. I don't ask the right questions and I never find the right answers."

"Neither do I."

"You could have had your pick of chaperones, and you chose one ranked fifty-second out of fifty-two." She kicked at the glitter on the ground. "May I ask why?"

"It doesn't matter," I said. "I was asking the wrong questions, too. Hangfire's been using us from the beginning, to advance his schemes. The theft of the Bombinating Beast, the disappearance of Cleo Knight, the burning of Stain'd Secondary School—all of our big cases have turned out to

143

be part of Hangfire's treachery, and we're still no closer to defeating him."

"All the more reason to leave town," Theodora said. "We can be transferred to another location, and we'll never have to worry about Stain'd-by-the-Sea again."

"And what will happen to the people here?"

"Don't think about them," she said to me. "Think about your sister, Snicket."

The room spun a little. It's like that when you are shocked. "What do you mean?" I said.

"You know precisely what I mean," she said. "If we return to the city, maybe we can get her out of prison."

"You have no way of knowing that."

"I know that if we don't leave she won't be saved."

"You don't know that, either," I said. "My sister is very brave and very resourceful."

"Some of the bravest and most resourceful people in the world have come to bad ends,"

Theodora said, and rubbed her cheek. I watched her. It was tempting to leave town. I wanted to do it. My empty suitcase was under the bed, watched over by the painting of the girl with the dog with the bandaged paw. There were very few things I wanted to bring with me. I looked at the bruise on Theodora's cheek and thought about the bandage on Moxie's arm. People getting hurt was one reason I never should have come to this town, I thought. But it was also the reason to stay. I leaned down on the floor and hoisted something from under the bed, but it wasn't my suitcase. It was a small box with a funnel growing out of it and a crank clinging to its side.

Theodora frowned. "You're making the wrong choice, Snicket. As your chaperone, I am obliged to warn you of this."

"And as your apprentice, I am obligated to remind you that I am under your supervision. You can't leave town without me."

"I'll drag you out of here if I have to."

"You and your gal pal?" I couldn't help saying, and pointed at the splinters of yellow on her fingernails. "You may not be able to trust your friends, but I can trust mine."

"You're *unsupervised*, Snicket," she said, as if Unsupervised were my first name. "I might be required to stay in town, but I'm not required to go wherever you are going."

"I wouldn't ask you to go with me," I said. "I only work with competent associates I can trust."

Theodora gasped, as if someone had struck her again. It was a rude thing I'd said to her. I had called her incompetent, which meant she couldn't do anything right. And I had called her untrustworthy, which meant I didn't know if she would even try to do the right thing. I couldn't decide if it was true, what I'd said about her. It was just something that had said itself. I didn't have time to worry about it.

"I'll have Prosper Lost send up some ice," I said. "Wrap some in a towel and hold it to your cheek while you're unpacking. It will reduce the swelling."

"Where are you going?"

"I'd like to see for myself the value of a top-drawer education," I said, and left with Ellington's old-fashioned phonograph under one arm and the library book she'd requested under the other. I walked down the stairs and told Prosper Lost about the ice, and then I went into the phone booth and called the Officers Mitchum. I asked Harvey how Qwerty was doing. Mimi said he was fine. I asked Mimi if I could talk to him, and Harvey said no. I asked Harvey if I could talk to him later, and Mimi said nobody could talk to Dashiell Qwerty and that he would be locked up until the train arrived to take him into the city. Both of them asked me why I was asking all these questions, and I said it was because I was finally interested in becoming a schoolchild like their adorable son Stew and then I asked both of them if Stew got his adorable qualities from his mother or from his father and then I let the phone dangle when they started to argue over it and walked out of the lobby feeling a little bit better.

It was still hot. The rain was closer. I lugged the phonograph over to Hungry's, and out in front was the Bellerophon brothers' taxicab, just as I'd hoped. It was empty, just as I hadn't. I put the phonograph in the back and then went inside. The Bellerophon brothers were there. They looked pale and sickly, but Hungry was yelling at them anyway. "Go on, get out of here!" she said, shooing them with a rag. "You're not getting another free meal from us."

"Be a sport, Hungry," Pip said. "We could eat a horse."

"We haven't had anything for almost three days," Squeak said.

"Go whine about it to Jake, if you can find him," Hungry said.

"He's at school," I told her.

She frowned. "He doesn't need any more learning. He reads too much as it is."

"It wasn't his idea," I reassured her.

"Well, he should have told me," she said. "He promised me he'd be right back. I've been worrying about him."

I looked at her face and saw it was true. Like Prosper Lost, she was a nicer person when she talked about people she loved.

"I last saw Jake getting into a van marked DEPARTMENT OF TRUANCY," I said.

Hungry shook her head. "Never heard of it."

I turned to the brothers. "But you have."

Pip and Squeak looked at each other and then at me. "We've been hiding out from them," Pip said. "Twice that van has chased us all over town, and we couldn't risk it again. We parked and lay low for a few days, but our stomachs were growling."

"No food at home?"

"Our father is still very ill," Squeak squeaked.

"Let me take care of you," I said, and walked behind the counter.

"You can't do that!" Hungry said. "This is my place! It's private property!"

"What it is is a kitchen," I said, "and these are hungry people. Hungry people should be fed. It takes some people a long time to figure this out, so you think about it and have a seat. I'll make enough for everybody."

I poured the brothers some juice from a pitcher. If you haven't eaten in a while, it's good to start with juice. I opened the refrigerator and took out what I could find, which was chicken and tomatoes and green peppers and plain, smooth yogurt. I looked at them for a second. Cooking isn't very difficult. You just take edible things and turn them into something you want to eat. I turned on the grill so it'd be hot when I needed it, and I looked around for some rice and found some and put it in a pot of water on the stove. I put the yogurt in a bowl and found where

Jake kept his spices and shook out coriander and cumin and ginger and cardamom and cinnamon and cayenne. I chopped the tomatoes and the green peppers and the chicken, and I mixed it up in the spiced yogurt and then spread it out on the grill to cook. Pip and Squeak looked a little better with the juice in them. The chicken and the vegetables changed color in the heat. I checked to make sure the chicken was cooked, and it was, so I found four plates and divvied up the rice and put the food on top.

"Dig in," I told everybody.

"What is it?" Hungry asked.

"Tandoori chicken with vegetables," I said. "Sort of. Real tandoori chicken is cooked in a special oven, in India and other countries where they're not afraid of spices."

"You don't have to tell me that," Hungry said. "I married a man from Calcutta."

"How'd that work out?" I asked.

"None of your business," Hungry said, with

151

her mouth full. Pip and Squeak didn't say anything. They ate furiously. It is a nice feeling to
watch people enjoy what you've made for them.
A root beer would have made it better, but
Stain'd-by-the-Sea just didn't seem to have one.
Not even one lonely bottle. There is no justice in
this town, I thought, letting the pots soak.

"That hit the spot," Pip said, when it was
over. "That hit two spots, Snicket. Thank you
very much."

"You're welcome very much," I said.

Squeak wiped his mouth and said thanks,
too. "Now what can we do for you?"

"I need a ride," I said. "I already put some
stuff in back."

"Of course," Pip said. "Let's go."

Hungry licked her spoon and then pointed
it at me. "Aren't you forgetting the dishes?" she
asked.

"Absolutely not," I said. "I'll remember the

dishes as long as I live. See you later, Hungry. If all goes well, I'll bring Jake back to you very soon."

We left and got in the car. Squeak got down on the floor so he could work the pedals for the gas and the brakes, and Pip sat on a stack of books and adjusted the rearview mirror. "Where to?" he asked me.

I told them.

"You mean you want to go exactly where the Department of Truancy wanted to take us?" Squeak said.

"I'm afraid so," I said.

"That's dangerous and it's far," Pip said. "It's a long way from home."

"I'm already a long way from home," I said. "I'm probably going to get even farther from home before I see my family again."

"It's hard when you're missing your family," Pip said, and started up the motor. "You wake up every morning like someone took one of your legs. All right, Snicket. We'll take you. But I hope you have a big tip ready."

I'd been saving one. The agreement I had with the Bellerophon brothers meant I recommended a book to them for every ride they gave me, instead of money, which I didn't have. "There's a book I really like," I said, "that begins on a dark and stormy night," and Squeak hit the gas and we got going. I told them all about the book. In most cases I wouldn't have told the whole story, but I went through every detail, from the scientist who disappears mysteriously to the frighteningly intelligent boy, from the haunted house to the curious woman with the crystal ball to the terrifying black cloud and the brain that can talk all by itself. It was a long ride to the Wade Academy, and we were nervous about going there. The story of the book filled the car with exciting adventures of the sort that are fun to read about, so we didn't have to think about the exciting adventures of the sort that are no fun to live through.

The taxi made its way down the bumpy path that had once been a cliff overlooking the sea. It was the way I had first come to town, staring out the window of Theodora's roadster at the bare, grim landscape of the ink industry, full of giant mechanized needles poking their way into deep wells where the area's last octopi still lived and inked. Beyond that was the wild and lawless Clusterous Forest, with the wind rippling through the seaweed that had somehow survived the draining of the sea, looking as mysterious as it did on the day I arrived. With the sea gone, Offshore Island was just a pile of stones rising from the bare seafloor, with an eerie bridge hanging over the missing water, and a rickety platform that had once served as a stop for the train. The Bellerophons had to circle around the bridge to find a route to rattle us over the shoreline and up toward Wade Academy. The bell rang as we approached the faded brick wall that surrounded the school. The sound was louder than I'd ever heard it, or maybe I was just closer than I'd ever been. Pip reached over and opened the glove compartment.

"I have some of those masks in here," he told me.

"I thought we didn't really need them," Squeak said from below.

"We want to look like people who think we need them," I said, and Pip passed them around. It was dark inside the mask. My breath wheezed through the mechanism at the mouth. All three of us wheezed together in the car, as if we were fighting for our lives. Outside, the brick wall loomed over us like an eager dentist, casting a deep shadow over the taxi and the three nervous people inside. I could see a large pile of something, gathered together in a spot right near the wall. The pile was round and tall like a haystack, made of something leafy, or something papery. I looked closer, but I couldn't see what it was.

"We're here," Pip said, his voice muffled behind his own mask.

"We certainly are," I said.

"What now?" Squeak asked.

"Now," I said, "you wish me luck."

The Bellerophons looked at each other. "'Wish me luck,' he says," Pip said to his brother, "like we're just going to drop him off at this sinister place and go home and suck our thumbs."

"I need you in town," I said. "Whatever Hangfire is cooking up here will be brought to Stain'd-by-the-Sea. You two are the last competent and trustworthy people I know who aren't locked up in one way or another. I want you to go back to town and see if you catch wind of anything. You can meet me back here in the morning and we can share information."

"What if you need to get to town before then?"

"I'll walk."

"They might be watching the roads."

I looked up at the strange landscape and saw the lighthouse looking back at me from the top of the cliffs. "If I have to," I said, "I can climb back up there using safety ropes I can fashion from seaweed."

Squeak crawled up from his position on the floor to look at me. "Someday," he said, "you'll have to tell us where you learned to do all these difficult things."

"I bet it's no more difficult than learning to drive," I told them, and got out of the taxi. The ground was so steep and uneven that I was unsteady for a moment, the way you are when you get out of bed after a nightmare. I grabbed the phonograph and felt it want to roll away as far as it could go. Part of me wanted to do the same. But instead I tried to give the Bellerophon brothers a smile, before realizing they couldn't see it behind the mask. I knocked on the hood of the car instead. They understood, I think. In any case, they drove away and left me.

I looked up at the wall. It was like standing at a towering, dull-looking book. I skipped ahead a few chapters until I found an iron gate that looked cold and threatening and very, very locked. But with the gentlest of pushes it groaned its way open on hinges that were a complicated arrangement of grinding gears. It was the sort of mechanism my sister would have admired.

Don't think of her now, I thought.

When I stepped through, I was in a jagged landscape of big rocks and small shrubs. It stretched out very far. It looked like a desert, but the air still felt rainy. I felt sweat at the back of my neck, and on my face under the mask, and on my palms as I kept switching the phonograph to alternate hands, and then everywhere as I walked toward the school. The Wade Academy's buildings were blank and brick. Here and there were slender windows, but there weren't enough of them for my taste. The place looked like it was sleeping. It was even quieter than Stain'd Secondary, before it had burned down, and schools should not be quiet places. It was wrong. The only sounds I heard were my own awkward footsteps and the whirs and clicks of the sort of insects that show up in warm weather as dusk approaches. Each sort of insect has a different sort of noise it uses for communication, although to me all the noises sounded like they were telling me to do something else.

Wait until evening, I told myself. It'll be dark soon. Only a fool would approach this school in the daytime. Of course, only a fool would be here to begin with. Maybe it's nothing. Maybe this school is perfectly harmless. Then why don't you just walk right in there? Oh, leave me alone. I argued with me for a while and decided that I was right. I should wait. Behind a few shrubs was a large, abandoned wagon, longer than an automobile and wider, too. It looked like something a farmer might use, or people who traveled with all the books they owned, just in case they needed one of them. It was a good place to wait. When the light grew too dim to read *Caviar: Salty Jewel of the Tasty Sea*, I put it in my shirt for safekeeping, and passed the rest of the time trying to remember everything that happens to a little bunny who appeared in books I didn't like. He disobeys his mother and eats vegetables out of some man's garden. He loses his jacket and shoes. He drinks chamomile tea. He gets his clothes cleaned by a hedgehog. He gathers onions. He helps his sister Flopsy. Before I knew it, it was dark.

I stood up. The insects were louder and the school seemed quieter. I could only see one light on in the whole place, flickering in front of a window. The phonograph felt heavier, and I kept stumbling on roots and rocks in the dark, but I tried to make my way closer to the light. It was impossible to know if the light was a good sign or a bad sign, if I was wise to walk toward it or if I'd be wiser to walk away from it. I couldn't even be sure it was a light. It might have been just a small, round reflection, something shiny in a window. This, too, reminded me of something. I'd almost figured out what it was when I heard a noise behind me.

It was too late, though. I was already walloped, hard, on the head.

The world went dizzy. I dropped the phonograph and heard it smash, but it took me about a week to fall down myself. Who hit me? I thought. Flopsy? Mopsy? Harold Limetta? And then my body hit the stones on the ground and everything hurt and everything got darker. A blow like this, I thought to myself, is likely to make you unconscious. You might be unconscious now, Snicket. You're already lying on the ground.

A shadow fell over me. I wasn't unconscious yet. I could see eyes, blinking in the little slits in a mask.

"I think you should be in school," the voice said.

I couldn't answer, so I didn't. The eyes blinked at me and I heard the *pitter-pat pitter-pat* on my mask and felt drops on my skin. The rain had finally begun. I took it personally. The mask bent closer—closer—

CHAPTER EIGHT

"We don't have any ice," I heard myself say, in a voice that was strange for me. My mask was off and my eyes were closed. I tried to breathe, but something sweet stuck in my throat. "Ice would reduce the swelling," I was saying, "but all I have is this washcloth soaked in cold water."

Something clammy lay down on my forehead. "I need you to wake up, Snicket," I said, and sighed. The sigh helped the sweet smell slither deeper down into me. I didn't like it and it reminded me of something. The Hemlock Tearoom and Stationery Shop, I thought. Those people pretending to be your parents. You fell asleep there and your entire time in Stain'd-by-the-Sea has been a dream. Go back to sleep. I told myself I was right and it was a good idea and then something startling was under my nose.

"Wake up," I said, loudly now. Whatever was under my nose chased the sweet smell away. Now I smelled dirt and cinnamon and it made me cough. The clammy washcloth pressed down on my forehead and I frowned and opened my eyes.

I saw a big poster shouting LEARNING IS FUN! It was a fine time to bring that up.

"Are you awake?" I asked me, but it wasn't me who was talking. It hadn't been all along. I turned my head and ached and blinked and found myself staring into a pair of green eyes. They blinked below a pair of eyebrows curled up like question marks, and after she blinked, the girl gave me a smile that might have meant anything.

"Lemony Snicket," she said.

"Ellington Feint," I said. Her hair was black again—last I'd seen her it had been blond, so she could disguise herself as Cleo Knight. It was longer now, and twisted into two skinny braids that looked like sleeping snakes.

"Don't call me Ellington Feint," she said, and put down a handkerchief she was holding. It was knotted to hold something that she'd put under my nose to wake me up. "Here I'm using a different name. I've registered at the Wade Academy under the name Filene N. Gottlin."

"That's scarcely believable," I said.

"I changed the letters around in 'Ellington Feint' so my assumed name would be an anagram of my real one. I suppose you could think of a better one?"

"Lifelong Intent," I said. "Entitling Felon. No Flint Gentile. I've been thoroughly trained in anagrams. But that's not what I meant. I mean it's hard to believe you've enrolled in this school. Do you know what goes on here?"

"I'm trying to find out," Ellington said. "I'm not here for a top-drawer education, Snicket. I'm here to find my father."

"What makes you think he's here?"

Ellington frowned, and walked away from where I lay. I sat up and, taking the wet washcloth off my aching head, took my first good look around. I was in a small, plain room, containing little more than a desk, a chair, a set of drawers, and the poster on the wall. There was a sink with a mirror bolted above it that reflected my bruised and tired face, and there was one small window with rain rattling against the pane and two items sitting on the sill: a dented pair of binoculars and a flowerpot with some leaves growing out of it that looked sickly. Ellington had crossed to a scuffed door and had pressed her ear against it, listening. I didn't hear anything, but as I listened I realized I was lying in Ellington's bed, with her blankets tucked tightly around me. It was a strange feeling, to be tucked into her bed. I don't know how to describe it. I'm not sure anyone could.

"I thought I heard him coming," Ellington said.

"Who?"

"Stew Mitchum. He polices these hallways day and night with a cigarette in his mouth and a smirk on his face."

"There's boys like that at every school."

Ellington gave me a small smile and walked over to the window. "I saw him attack you," she said, gesturing to the binoculars, "but he didn't have the strength to drag you inside. He went to get help and I took a chance and snuck out."

"Thank you for rescuing me," I said, and put the washcloth back on my forehead. I could feel a bump growing there, like a cake rising in the oven, but I wasn't thinking about the bump.

I was thinking about Ellington Feint, dragging me to her room. She was stronger than Stew Mitchum, or maybe she just wanted something more than he did. Or maybe, Snicket, I thought to myself—

"Thank you for bringing back my phonograph," she said, "though I'm afraid it got smashed up as badly as you did."

"I'm sorry to hear that," I said, "but I brought you something else."

I reached under the blanket and unbuttoned my shirt. Ellington didn't say anything until I brought the book out. She didn't say anything then, either. But her face changed. It changed like water on a piece of paper, growing darker and sadder.

"You don't have to say anything," I said. "I'll say it for you. You wanted to read this book for the same reason I did. We were both investigating the process by which caviar is made. But by the time we found out about Roe House,

Hangfire had set up his fraudulent Department of Education. Before long, all the town's school-children had been transferred here, and Dashiell Qwerty was arrested for arson."

Ellington gasped. "Qwerty's been arrested?"

"He gave me this book right before the Mitchums took him away, and he'll be on the train to the city soon for his trial."

"There's more to a library than the librarian," Ellington said. "At least the information in the library is still safe."

"We shouldn't underestimate the villainy of a villain," I said. "Just by lighting a few fires, Hangfire managed to get a powerful librarian out of his way and all of the town's school-children in his clutches. He killed two birds with one stone."

Ellington turned and gave me a sad smile, and then she reached over to the bed and slipped her hand underneath the mattress to find something. She brought out an object I had seen once before. It was about the size of a deck of cards, with a tiny funnel and a small crank that she wound quickly before putting it on the pillow next to me. It played a melody I always liked to hear, whether from her phonograph or from this small thing, the music box her father had given her. "Two birds with one stone," Ellington repeated, over the tinkly music. "My father always hated that expression. He said nobody should be throwing any stones at any birds."

"He sounds like a very gentle person."

"He is. He doesn't belong in a place like this."

"Have you seen him here?"

Ellington shook her head. "And they've confiscated the one hope I had of finding him. It's gone, Snicket. The woman who runs this place took it away along with almost everything else, as soon as I arrived at the Wade Academy. It's all I had that could lead me to my father."

"The Bombinating Beast," I said, and nodded grimly. We kept quiet for a minute, with only the music for company. I picked up the music box and looked at it, although it was the statue I really wanted to see. I imagined the scales carved into its slender, wooden body, and its toothy, empty grin, and the odd crinkly patch of paper that was stretched over a small hole at its base. But most of all I pictured the statue's empty, hollow eyes. As I pictured its gaze, my fingers fumbled with the music box, and I found myself winding the crank the opposite way. The music continued, but there was another sound underneath it, a little whir of gears and then a small, bright *click!* as a panel on the music box opened and a small piece of paper tumbled out into my hand. I turned it over. It wasn't a piece of paper. It was a photograph, a small one, of a man with kind eyes, frowning at me. Ellington leaned over my shoulder to see.

There's no way to tell what will make someone break down in tears. There are some who will cry at the merest melancholy word, and there are some who need the longest, cruelest speech to even dampen one eyelash. There are those who will cry at any sad song but no sad book, and there are those who are immune to the most saddening newspaper articles but will weep for days over a terrible meal. People cry at silence or at violence, in a graveyard or a school-yard. It is always a puzzle, and for Ellington Feint the unexpected photograph of her father made her hang her head and sob into her hands. I let her cry. She wasn't alone. I put the damp washcloth to my forehead so she wouldn't know I was crying too. Everyone tells you it's all right to cry, but not enough people say it's all right if you don't want people to know. The rain rattled on the window like it was also crying and then finally everything fell silent.

"I'm sorry," she said.

"It's all right to cry."

"There are lots of things that are all right, but I don't like to do them in front of other people." She held the tiny photograph in her hands. "Will I ever see him again, Snicket?"

"Anytime you open the music box," I said.

"You know what I mean."

"Ask me after a good night's sleep," I said, and rubbed the bump on my forehead.

She snapped her fingers and hurried to the sink. She turned on the water and splashed some on her face and then let it run until it began to steam. She opened a drawer of the desk and took out two white cups. She grabbed the knotted handkerchief she'd used to wake me up and then fussed with all these things in the basin of the sink and then finally handed me one steaming cup and sipped from the other one.

"It's not the best way to make coffee," she said, "but it's the only way I can do it here."

"I don't drink coffee," I reminded her.

"You're going to start," she told me. "Don't you smell it, Snicket? That sickly sweet smell that's everywhere?"

I nodded. "I recognize it from somewhere," I said. "It's on the tip of my tongue."

"I hope not," Ellington said. "It's laudanum, a chemical that makes you sleepy."

"Of course," I said. "It's what Dr. Flammarion used on Cleo Knight's parents." I did not add that I'd narrowly escaped it myself, in the city some months back and, it felt, a thousand years ago.

"It's what Hangfire's using on everyone," Ellington said. "You can smell it everywhere here, and it keeps the students sleepy and confused. Coffee helps fight the effects."

"Then I'm surprised they didn't confiscate the coffee," I said.

"They would have," Ellington said, "but I hid it."

I looked around. "Where?"

"In plain sight, Snicket. That's not soil in that flowerpot."

"No wonder the plant looks so miserable."

"Drink up, Snicket."

She handed me the mug. I didn't want to drink up. I also didn't want to be in this sinister place. I didn't want my sister in prison. I didn't want my head hurt and my clothes wet with rain. I made a whole list of things in my head that I didn't want, and then I wondered exactly what I could do with such a list, and I closed my eyes and took a gulp of coffee. It tasted like a hot, melted tire. I was embarrassed at the noises I made when I sipped it. I opened my eyes to see if Ellington had noticed and saw she was laughing at me.

"That's not nice," I said.

"You're right and I'm sorry," she said. "It's just good to see there's one thing I'm better at than you are."

"I think you're better at everything," I said. I hoped the second sip would be better. It wasn't. "I keep lurking around this mystery, but you walked right into the heart of it. I don't know how you find the nerve to do the things you've done."

"I only have the nerve," she said, "because I know you're always close behind me."

We sipped coffee. It was still awful, but there was something wonderful about sitting together and sipping even the bitterest of beverages. You cannot wait for an untroubled world to have an untroubled moment. The terrible phone call, the rainstorm, the sinister knock on the door—they will all come. Soon enough arrive the treacherous villain and the unfair trial and the smoke and the flames of the suspicious fires to burn everything away. In the meantime, it is best to grab what wonderful moments you find lying around. Ellington and I sipped and said nothing. The music box finished its tune and the photograph sat on the blanket between us. I didn't want to look at it any longer. The picture forced a question into my mouth that burned worse than the coffee. Don't ask it, I told myself, as the wonderful faded and I was left with a moment that was worsening and worsening. Ask another question. Don't ask the wrong question. "Ellington," I said finally—

"Filene."

"Filene—"

But there was a knock on the door. Ellington moved very quickly. She handed me her coffee and then ushered all three of us—me and the two cups—under the bed. The mattress hung low, and I had to lie very flat, with a steaming cup on each side. Something bumped against me, right at my right knee, but I didn't have time to see what it was, as Ellington pulled the blankets down so I was completely hidden. I listened to her stand there for just a second, surveying her handiwork, and then I heard her open the door, just a crack.

"Yes?"

"It's Sharon Haines," a voice said, and it was. *The woman who runs this place*, I thought. That's what Ellington had called her, as if she did not know the woman's name.

"I was just about to get into bed," Ellington said, with a fake yawn that wasn't bad.

"Don't sleep too long," Sharon said. "Tomorrow is a big day."

"I know."

"I'm counting on you. We all are."

"I *know*," Ellington said again, in a tone I recognized. She was tired of being told the same thing over and over again. You can hear this tone all over the world.

"Nothing can go wrong, Filene."

"People who think nothing can go wrong are usually disappointed."

"Stew tells me there's been an intruder."

"I wouldn't know anything about that."

"Stew knocked him unconscious, but then he disappeared."

"Well," Ellington said, "I'll be on the lookout

for an unconscious man wandering around the school grounds."

"Don't get smart," Sharon said, but she did not say it very well. Her voice was too trembly. "The intruder had a phonograph with him. It broke to pieces."

"You promised to take good care of that," Ellington said quietly, and then there was a pause. Nobody said anything, for no reason I could imagine. I felt the cups warm in my hands, and tried to move my head to take a look at whatever object was bumping against my knee. It was black, or maybe it was just dark under the bed. The pause continued. Maybe you're wrong, I told myself.

"The machine is broken," Sharon admitted finally, "but I still did my part. And I know he expects you to do yours."

"I will," Ellington said quietly, and the door clattered shut. I listened to Ellington listening at the door for Sharon's departing footsteps until it was time to say "All clear."

"All clear," she said, and raised the blanket like a curtain. I crawled out and gave her back her coffee and looked at her. It was simple, I thought. She was either working with Hangfire or she was pretending to. She was either helping out with a sinister scheme or just playing along to rescue her father. Now she was either going to tell me the truth or she was going to lie. There's a knock on your bedroom window in the middle of the night, and when you look outside there's someone just your age, or maybe a little older, who says they need your help. You either unlock the window and let them in or you don't. It's very simple, I thought. But the trouble is, it's not easy.

"I have a question," I said.

"I'm sure you have many questions," Ellington said, "but right now you need to finish your coffee or we'll be late."

"Late for what?"

"I'm not the only student who doesn't like this place," Ellington said. "There are other people here who aren't muddled by laudanum and a top-drawer education. We're meeting in the library to see what can be done."

I finished my coffee in one squirmy gulp. I felt the drink jitter its way through my system, like a secret code tapping its way down my spine. I didn't like it, but I didn't feel as sleepy as I had before. "The library in town?" I asked, wishing I hadn't sent Pip and Squeak away.

"No," Ellington said, "the school library. It's a safe place, but it's all the way across campus, so we'll have to watch out for Stew or anyone else in the Inhumane Society. Take your shoes and socks off, Snicket."

"Why?"

"Shoes make an awful racket in the hall-ways," she said, "and the floors are too slippery for socks."

"I'll take my chances," I said.

Ellington gave me a quizzical look as she kicked off her own shoes. Her toenails, I noticed, were painted as black as her fingernails, although they looked more startling on her slender feet. "If you attract attention, it could ruin our only chance to defeat Hangfire. Take off your shoes and socks."

I hesitated, sitting on the edge of the bed.

"Are you bashful, Snicket?"

"I'm not bashful."

"Do you have ugly toes? I promise not to say anything about them."

"My toes," I said, with as much dignity as I had lying around, "are perfectly normal, thank you very much."

"Then what is the problem?"

"There isn't one," I said, and I quickly pulled off my shoes. I had to lean down to do it, and I had another opportunity to look at the object under the bed as I peeled off my socks and dropped them to the floor. It felt good to get them off. They were wet from the rain. But taking my shoes and socks off left my ankles bare, and Ellington stared hard at one of them.

"Oh," she said.

"Oh," I agreed.

She leaned down and ran a finger along the tattoo on my ankle. To most people it looked like an eye, but hidden in the eye were three initials. They were not hidden to Ellington. She spelled them out with her fingernail on my skin.

"V.F.D.," she said.

"Yes."

"Volunteer Fire Department."

"Yes."

"That's another secret organization, isn't it?"

"If I told you," I said, "it wouldn't be a secret."

"That's why you're here in town," she said. "It's training of some kind, isn't it? That woman Theodora is your tutor or something."

"Chaperone, is what they call it."

"You're scattered all over the place," she said,

"doing secret errands and investigations, just like the Inhumane Society."

I shook my head. "Not like them at all."

"What's the difference?" Ellington asked.

I tried to think of the best way to put it. It was simple, I thought, looking at the library book, but it wasn't easy. It's like the difference between what happens in a book and what happens in the world. The world is swirling with so many mysteries and secrets that nobody will ever track down all of them. But with a book you can stay up very late, reading and rereading until all the secrets are clear to you. The questions of the world are hidden forever, but the answers in a book are hiding in plain sight.

"We read a lot," I said finally, and to my surprise Ellington Feint nodded like she understood. She opened the door to see if anyone was watching us, then took another quick look at the eye on my ankle. Then she beckoned me to follow her out the door and into the hallway. It was dim and quiet, and the scent of laudanum was in the air. But the coffee was in my blood, so I didn't feel sleepy. What I felt was curious. I was curious about what we were doing. I was curious about who we were meeting. And I was curious about the object under the bed. It wasn't black, I'd seen. It was just a dark green, a green bag in the shape of a tube, with a long zipper running down it like an open, toothy mouth. It was a good bag to hide things in. Last I'd seen it, it was hiding the Bombinating Beast.

CHAPTER NINE

The hallways of the Wade Academy were tricky for sneaking, but I'd had a very demanding sneaking instructor. Our final exam began early in the morning, with our instructor entering a small cabin in the middle of the woods and sitting blindfolded in a folding chair. The woods were full of crackly dead leaves, and the floor of the cabin was covered in fragile glass figurines. To pass the class we had to sneak up on him by midnight. When he arrived at the cabin that morning, the entire class was waiting for him. I'd snuck into his office the night before and shared the location of the cabin with the rest of the students so we could sneak up on him before he even arrived. I received the top grade in the class and a three-month suspension.

This was harder. I didn't know where Ellington Feint was going, or if I should have been following her to begin with. The hallways were dead empty, and if anyone happened upon us there was nowhere to hide, except perhaps by dashing through a door into possibly more dangerous circumstances. The floors were slightly sticky and slightly damp, and from the smell I gathered that they had been mopped with laudanum. At least half of the janitors you encounter in your life are working for the enemy. But there were plenty of noises to use as cover for our movements. There were thumps from below and creaks from above, as the other students at the

Wade Academy moved around in their rooms. From behind the doors we heard the occasional moan, or a loud snore, or the occasional muffled bout of confused weeping. There were no schoolchildren to be seen. There was only Ellington Feint and there was only me.

Ellington was good. She led the way on tiptoe, and could flatten herself against the wall for a long time without getting fidgety or bored. Her face remained calm as she led me through a maze of hallways and staircases. The only sign she was nervous was from her slender fingers, which kept moving up to fiddle with one of her braids. That left the other braid for me to fiddle with, but I did not think that was appropriate.

Twice we heard footsteps. Twice the footsteps faded away. My bare feet were cold on the floor.

At long last Ellington led me to a wide glass door marked LIBRARY and ushered me inside. It was one big room, and all of it was dark. I could see tall shelves, and a few windows covered in thick shades that hid the starlight. In the middle of the room was a circular table with shadows gathered around it.

"Who wrote *The Wind in the Willows*?" asked one of them.

"Who plays trumpet on *Out to Lunch*?" shot back Ellington.

There was an awkward pause in the dark.

"It's Kenneth Grahame," I offered finally. "And Freddie Hubbard on trumpet, I think."

"Who is that?" the voice asked.

Ellington sighed. "Kellar, turn on the light."

Kellar Haines turned on the light. I should have recognized his shadow by the dynamite spike of his hair. Next to him was a girl I did not recognize, a tall girl with a cap sitting backward on her head and a small square of paper pressed flat on the table. She had a cigarette in

her mouth, unlit. So did Kellar. So did Jake Hix.
So did Cleo Knight. The only person at the table
without a cigarette was a crumpled, half-asleep
figure that it took me a moment to recognize as
Moxie Mallahan.

"Don't you have any fire?" I asked.

"Snicket!" Cleo rose and clapped me on the
shoulder. "You're here!"

"That's a nasty lump you got yourself," Jake
said.

"It was a gift from a very adorable boy," I
told him.

Jake frowned in sympathy. "Stew's been
a brute to all of us," he said. "He would have
ripped up Moxie's notes, if Cleo hadn't kicked
him in the shins."

"We're having a pretty tough time here,
Snicket," Cleo said.

"It takes a while to adjust to a new school," I
said, "but that's no reason to take up smoking."

"These aren't cigarettes," Jake said, handing me his. "Cleo rigged something up for us that fights the effect of laudanum."

"One of the shrubs around here contains a nutrient that acts as a natural stimulant," Cleo explained. "If you chew on a rolled-up piece of bark, you don't feel as tired."

"That's a good idea," I said.

"It was someone else's good idea," Cleo said. "I found a rolled-up bark cigarette in the trash, near 350 Wayward Way."

"The bark's been stripped away from most of the shrubs," Jake said. "Someone has been out here fighting the effects of laudanum for quite some time."

"There's not enough to go around," Cleo said. "That's why Moxie's in such bad shape."

I gave Moxie a gentle nudge. "What's the news?"

Moxie's eyes fluttered. "I'm afraid I'm missing

most of it," she murmured, "but I'm glad to see you. I missed you too, Snicket."

Ellington took another knotted handker-chief out of her pocket. "If we can find water, I can make some coffee," she said. "That should sharpen us up a little."

"There's a sink behind the librarian's desk," Kellar said, and Ellington hurried toward her errand. The others looked at me, except Moxie, whose eyes were open but looking at nothing.

"I know Ellington hasn't always been trust-worthy," Cleo said, in a quiet murmur, "but without her coffee I'm not sure we'd be here talking to you."

"Tell me what's been going on," I said.

"Here's someone who knows more than we do," Jake said, gesturing to the girl I didn't know. "Snicket, this is Ornette Lost."

I shook the girl's hand and told her I knew her father.

"How is he?" she asked me.

"Worried about you."

"He should be," Ornette said. "Everyone should be worried about everyone here. After my school burned down, the Department of Education told us we'd get a top-drawer education, but everybody in the drawer is wandering around in a daze." She tilted the paper this way and that and in no time had a folded pyramid in front of her. She was quick with it, a marvel to watch. "This isn't a school," she said, and flicked the pyramid my way. "Not really. There are classrooms, but there aren't any classes. There are desks but no desk work. We were searched and told to stay in our rooms, and we stay there, and that's it and that's all."

"The occasional meal is left outside our doors," Kellar said, with a bitter shake of his head. "My mother was never a good cook, and now the food is laced with laudanum."

"This morning they made us unload a bunch

of equipment off a school bus," Ornette said, "and then drag it downstairs into a damp basement."

"What kind of equipment?" I asked her, and flicked the pyramid back to her.

"Fish tanks," she said.

"Small ones, about the size of a book?"

She shook her head. Now the pyramid was a ladder, leaning against her coffee cup. "Bigger than that."

We all looked at one another, all of us who knew, Jake and Cleo and Moxie. "It's the same plan as last time," I said in agreement. "He had the Colophon Clinic all ready to hold a number of children prisoner, along with a prominent naturalist and who knows who else. Now he's doing it at the Wade Academy. He's just switched from shackles to sleeping potion."

"But why?" Kellar asked. "What for?"

"I was hoping you could tell me," I said to him. "You and your mother are part of the plan."

Kellar sighed, and took an envelope out of

his pocket. He tipped it and a photograph fell out. Another photograph, I thought. Another sad story for a file full of them.

"This is my sister Lizzie," he said, and showed me a girl. She looked older than any of us, but it could just have been her glamorous dress. She had a wide and eager smile, and a long string of pearls around her neck she was fiddling with. "My sister was born for the stage," Kellar told us. "She always wanted to be an actress, and a few months ago she was invited to study with a theatrical legend here in Stain'd-by-the-Sea."

"Sally Murphy," I said.

Kellar's eyes grew even wider. "How did you know?"

"It's a long story," I said, referring to a volume you likely don't want to read.

"She was so happy to go," Kellar said, "but after a few months we stopped getting letters. We worried for a while, and then we heard from someone else."

"Hangfire," Moxie said, with a sleepy shudder.

Kellar nodded. "He told us that if we ever wanted to see Lizzie again, we had to follow his instructions exactly."

"All those fires," I said.

"We didn't burn those buildings down," Kellar said. "Tricking you and Theodora was our part. Someone else framed the librarian."

"You helped," Jake said. "You and your mother helped plenty."

"I know," Kellar said, "but we're desperate about my sister. She's all we have. We're the only ones who can help her."

He was wrong about that, but just then Ellington returned with coffee for everyone on a large, wide book she was using as a tray. "I found these mugs in a closet," she said, "and washed them out repeatedly in case they had laudanum in them. Drink up, everyone—but try to make it last. We're running low on coffee."

I drank up, and it wasn't hard to try to make

it last. Each sip was a mudslide in my mouth. I looked around at the table of wincing people. Only Ellington was enjoying her coffee, and I think she was also enjoying watching us not enjoy ours. Cleo helped Moxie drink from the mug, and the journalist's eyes began to flutter and focus around the room.

"So?" she said to me. "Have you figured out what Hangfire's up to?"

"I only heard Kellar's part of the plan," I said. "I haven't heard Ellington's."

Everyone at the table looked at Ellington Feint. She kept sipping. "My part?" she asked, in the tone of voice you use when you're standing next to a broken vase and don't want to be blamed for it.

"I heard every word of your conversation with Sharon Haines," I said. "Tomorrow's a big day, and she's counting on you. You said you'd do your part, and now you have to tell us what it is."

Ellington moved her mug to the center of the table. Her eyebrows, curved like question marks, felt like they belonged to all the questions in my mind, and then she gave me her smile, the one that might have meant anything. "It *is* a big day tomorrow," she said. "That Haines woman is driving all of the students into town for a field trip."

"A field trip?" Moxie repeated doubtfully.

"Most field trips contain sinister plots," I said.

Ellington nodded. "Hangfire needs something for whatever he's going to do in that basement. I don't know what it is, but everyone is being sent to help fetch it. Everyone but me."

"And what are you going to do?" I asked. "What's your part?"

"I'm supposed to climb to the top of the tower," Ellington said, "and ring the bell at one o'clock sharp."

"Why you?" Moxie asked.

"I got the job the way anyone gets an important job at school," Ellington answered. "I've been behaving sickeningly well."

"But why are you supposed to ring that bell?"

"I've been thinking about that," Ellington said. "I've been thinking about the reason for all the bell-ringing in Stain'd-by-the-Sea. I don't think it's to warn people about water pressure, or salt lung. Maybe it used to be. But now I think Hangfire rings the bell when he wants the town to be nervous and masked, so it's easier for him to skulk around."

"And where is he going to skulk," I wondered, "at one o'clock tomorrow?"

Ellington shook her head. "I don't know, but he won't be back until very late."

Kellar gave her a curious look. "Did he tell you this himself?"

Ellington turned to face him, and they stared

at each other for a moment, the two people in the room who had helped Hangfire in order to help someone else. I didn't like them together. It was like watching a lit match near a book. "No," she said.

"Who told you, then?" Kellar asked.

"Your mother," Ellington replied sharply. "I haven't seen hide nor hair of Hangfire since I arrived."

"Maybe he doesn't need to see you," I said, "now that he has the statue he needs."

"You gave it to him?" Moxie sputtered, looking at Ellington in astonishment.

"I had no choice," Ellington said quietly. "It was confiscated from me when I enrolled here. Tomorrow, while everyone else is in town, I'm going to search every inch of Wade Academy and Offshore Island for my father. Maybe if I can rescue him, Hangfire's plot will be ruined, and the Bombinating Beast won't matter."

"What's the Bombinating Beast?" Ornette asked, and I was sad to shake my head in reply.

"I still don't know," I admitted, and looked around the room. "I need to spend more time in the library."

"Not in this library," Jake said with a grimace, as if one of his recipes hadn't worked out. "See for yourself."

I stood up and saw for myself. The first book I plucked from the shelf had a plain cover, which is not too unusual at a library. The first few pages were blank, which is not too unusual in a book. But then everything was blank, each page as white and empty as an iceberg, and this is unusual everywhere but a paper factory. The others at the table watched me. It did not take long to see that all the books were the same. It made my eyes ache.

"I couldn't believe it either," Kellar said. "I have no idea why they would do such a thing."

"At first glance, this looks like a real library,"

I said, "just like Wade Academy looks like a top-drawer school. I guess Hangfire wanted to fool any parent who might have come to check on their child."

"Snicket," Moxie said quietly, "what are we going to do?"

"Not what everyone's parents did," I said. "Not nothing."

My associates looked at me, and I felt very weary. It wasn't only the laudanum's doing. My life felt heavy that night, with each year of my life like a weighty crate, so I had almost thirteen crates to carry around inside me, with each crate full of notebooks and each notebook full of secrets. It is hard to lug such a heavy load around with me and to keep everyone from seeing it. But some secrets are so strange and so dangerous that showing them to people makes the strangeness and the danger pour into their lives like dark, dark ink. I lived with this ink myself, emblazoned on my ankle for me to see each morning when I got out of bed, except for the days when I collapsed exhausted with my shoes on. But I did not want to stain anyone else's life. Moxie still had a bandage on her arm, and all the others at the table were exhausted and desperate creatures, caught in a web of Hangfire's devising, saved only by chewing on the bark of shrubs and drinking coffee filtered through a handkerchief. I did not want to burden them further. But the treachery of the world will continue no matter how much you worry about it, my sister had said to me. So I put my foot up on the table.

"What is that?" Cleo said, after a pause.

Jake leaned forward and frowned. "It's an eye," he said. "No, wait. It's initials."

"V.F.D.," Moxie said. "Is that real?"

"As real as literature," I said.

"What's V.F.D.?" Cleo asked.

"It's a secret organization," Moxie said. "I've seen mentions of it here and there."

"V.F.D. stands for Volunteer Fire Department," I said.

"So you put out fires?" Kellar asked.

"When we can," I said, "but there's more to it than that. We try to do what good we can in the world."

Jake frowned. "Doesn't everybody try to do that?"

"Not enough people," I said.

"I don't understand this," Moxie said. "What is it, exactly, that you do? What does V.F.D. believe?"

"We believe in an aristocracy," I said.

Moxie wanted to type so badly that she rattled her fingers on the table. "Doesn't that mean people who are rich and powerful?"

"Not that kind of aristocracy," I said, with both feet on the floor. "Not an aristocracy of power, based on rank or wealth, but an aristocracy of the sensitive, the considerate, and the plucky. Our members are found in all nations and classes, and all through the ages, and there is a secret understanding between us when we meet."

"Like us," Cleo said. "We've all read *The Wind in the Willows*, so we decided to use that as a code."

"Exactly," I said, watching Ellington frown out of the corner of my eye. "We represent the true human tradition, the one permanent victory over cruelty and chaos. We're an invincible army, but not a victorious one. We've had different names throughout history, but all the words that describe us are false and all attempts to organize us fail. Right now we're called V.F.D., but all our schisms and arguments might cause us to disappear. It won't matter. People like us always slip through the net. Our true home is the imagination, and our kingdom is the wide-open world."

It was quite a speech, and I'm not ashamed to say that most of it was paraphrased, a word which here means "more or less stolen from another one of my associates." But Edward had always managed to capture everyone's attention when he made that speech, and sure enough when I was done I could tell everyone was nodding silently. I took another sip and realized I was trembling.

"Can we join?" Cleo said finally.

"It seems to me you already have joined," I said.

"I hope that doesn't mean we have to get tattoos," Moxie said.

"I've never liked this," I said, frowning at my ankle. "It is unwise to make something permanent when the whole world is shifting. There may be a time when this symbol means something treacherous and terrible, rather than something noble and literate."

"And there may be a time," Cleo said darkly, "when our town disappears altogether, and Stain'd-by-the-Sea only survives as a name for Hangfire's villainous deeds."

"Not if we stop him," I said. "But right now we'd better scatter. This has been a long meeting, and we have a big day tomorrow."

"You mean we're actually going to go on that field trip?" Jake asked.

"Of course," I said. "I have a taxi to catch tomorrow, but the rest of you should get on that school bus. Keep your eyes and ears open and then meet up and share information."

"When will we meet?" Cleo asked.

"And where?" Moxie said.

"Hungry's," I said. "Just after one o'clock. Ellington will ring the bell, so it'll be easier to skulk away."

"So I guess we'll see each other on the school bus tomorrow morning," Moxie said, and we all nodded quietly. I couldn't help smiling. I hadn't realized how much I had missed attending secret meetings just like this one. We left the way V.F.D. always ended meetings—separately, quietly, and with firm handshakes. Cleo went out first, then Jake, then Ornette, then Moxie, and then Kellar, whose handshake felt strange in my palm.

"I feel like this is all my fault, Snicket," he said. "That's why I tried to give you messages about what was really happening. I knew helping Hangfire was the wrong thing to do, but you know how it is, arguing with a difficult mother."

"You did everything you could think of," I told him.

"I hope I'm still doing that," he said, still gripping my hand. "I'd like to think you can trust absolutely all of us. Well, good night."

I told him good night and he went out and I held tight to the object Kellar Haines had just slipped me. It was small, round, and cold, like a very thick coin. *I'd like to think you can trust absolutely all of us,* he'd said, so I thought it was best not to look at it in front of Ellington Feint. It occurred to me suddenly to wonder if I would spend the night tucked into her bed again.

"I know it's been a long night, Snicket," Ellington said to me, "but there's something else I need to show you."

"Is that so?" I asked.

"It is so."

Maybe this is her part, I thought. Maybe this is something else she promised Hangfire she'd do. "Lead the way," I said, and she did, sneaking down staircases, sneaking down hallways, sneaking through doors, until we were outside in the night and at once I knew I was in the wrong place.

The air was still warm, and the rain had slowed to a spit. The ground was hot slush beneath my bare feet. A watery moon was out,

but only half of it showed up in the overcast sky. A cloud drifted in front of it, with jagged edges like teeth, and the insects were still hissing in the crowded air. It was dark, but not so dark that I could not see Ellington's green eyes as she leaned in to murmur to me.

"Do you see that big rock"—and here she pointed with one finger that disappeared in the darkness—"way over there, that looks like the mouth of some weird animal?"

I saw that big rock, way over there, that looked like the mouth of some weird animal.

"There's a fire pond over there," she said. "That's where we're headed."

"Fire pond?" I said, and wished I had not sounded so quivery.

"A deep pit of water," she said. "Isolated places have them in case of fire, because there are no hydrants around. There's something I need to show you there. Come on."

She stepped nimbly out of sight. I had to follow her to see her. Good idea, I told myself. Follow a girl who has brought you nothing but trouble, toward a deep pit of water in an isolated location in the dark of night. If you were a book, Snicket, you would throw yourself down because your hero was acting foolishly. The Bombinating Beast is under her bed, Snicket, and you're following her into the darkness. You're unsupervised, Snicket, as Theodora would have told me. You're unsupervised and you're scared.

Get scared later, I told myself.

Myself told me very rude things in return.

We walked in silence across the grounds of Wade Academy, with its rocks and roots of shrubs and the chatter of worried insects. We headed steadily toward the mouth of some strange animal. My feet got dirty and sore. Ellington's slender shadow teetered in front of me as she moved across the landscape. We passed an awkward shape in the darkness that revealed itself, when I was close enough. It was a well, like the one Hangfire had used in the basement of the Sallis mansion, when he tried to drown Sally Murphy. I thought of Kellar's sister then, and my own. What will happen? I kept asking myself, but I knew it was the wrong question.

We reached the rock and then quietly, slowly, made our way around it. There was the fire pond, or at least I knew it to be there. It looked like nothing, just a large circle of rocks around a blackness so dark that I felt like I was floating just looking at it. The question was, how much trouble are you in? and the answer was I didn't know. Nobody ever does.

Ellington put her hand on my shoulder and guided me to the very edge of the rock, like it was a diving board. I could feel the nothingness of the dark pond, just under the tips of my toes, and Ellington's fingers on my shoulder.

If she pushes you, I thought, at last you will know. All of the reading and thinking you have done has pointed you toward a mystery of unspeakable size, and here it is, Snicket. Here's the dark thing you imagine very late, on very terrible nights. It has been beckoning you since you were a baby, when you emerged from the darkness of the womb. You didn't know it then, but from that moment on you would float toward another darkness, all the mysterious days and all the mysterious nights of your whole mysterious life. Here it is, Snicket. Listen for this mystery that has been stalking you since they first inked your ankle.

These thoughts did not appear out of thin air. They had a cause somewhere. All of the insects had stopped.

I held my breath in the quiet night until I couldn't stand it anymore, and then I did it much longer. Then, slowly, there was something else. It began far away, far enough that at first I thought the insects had started up again, with a dull buzzing appearing in the far corners of the air. I thought of the growl I'd heard from Stew Mitchum, outside Black Cat Coffee, and then it was louder. Maybe he'd gotten better at it. Maybe it wasn't him. Maybe it wasn't anyone. I thought of the hum of the engine of the Dilemma. Maybe it was a machine. It grew louder, fiercer, chopping the air like the spinning blades of a propeller, but rougher, and wetter, so that I decided it was no machine. It was something from the earth or the sky or the sea, or from a dream or the pages of a book I wasn't yet old enough to read, about monsters I wasn't brave enough to face. Soon it was an immense noise that rattled everything in my body. It was the sound of being chased in a nightmare, or the blind and violent fury of a bad parent, a tantrum that deafened the ears of the living and slithered across the bones of the dead. I felt its breath storm against me, filling my nose and my mouth with something salty and briny and my head and heart with fear and dread. It was real breathing, billowing in and out with a growling hunger and a growing rage, and real claws scraping against the rocks until they broke apart to scatter small pieces into the splashy depths below. It roared again. It wanted to do worse. But all it did was pour itself into the water, which churned and buzzed around it, and then with one ghastly gasp it was deep underwater and the last of its tail shook against a shrub and it was gone. The water bubbled after it and then stopped. It's gone, I told myself, but nothing moved for a long time. Finally the insects started talking again. I'm sure they were asking what it was and where it had come from and when they would see it again. I listened to the air, full of their questions, but I only had one question myself.

"Why didn't it attack us?" I said to Ellington.

Her hand trembled and stopped on my shoulder, trembled and stopped. She wasn't certain, but she had an answer. I waited for it in the dark.

"It's not old enough," she said finally.

CHAPTER TEN

Coffee or creature, I was wide awake when we got back to Ellington's room. My frightened teeth had chattered all the way, and I let them do all the talking. Not until Ellington had closed the door and we were alone in her room did I venture to say anything out loud.

"Was that real?" I asked.

"I don't know." Ellington sat down on the bed. Her green eyes looked very far away. "For a while I thought it was a nightmare," she said quietly. "It seemed wherever I went, there was something lurking around me—something dark and sinister that I could scarcely see."

I slumped to the floor and sat leaning against Ellington's desk. "I've had that feeling since I arrived in town," I said.

Ellington nodded. "Whenever I seem to get close to finding my father, I hear that horrible *thing*."

I thought of the terrible noises in the dark. Now, in Ellington's room, it seemed that they could not have been possible. "It must be a trick of Hangfire's," I said. "He's capable of imitating anyone's voice. He tricked me with a tape recording. Maybe he's trying to make us think there's a monster out there, so we don't investigate any further."

"Some sort of decoy, maybe," Ellington said thoughtfully.

I nodded. "So we won't ask the questions we should be asking."

Ellington hugged her knees to her chest. She looked much younger than she was, and her question sounded like a very young child's. "When will I see him again?" she asked. "When will I find my father?"

There was a difficult pause. "I don't know when you'll see him again," I said, when it was over, "but you can't give Hangfire what he wants, even if you lose your father forever."

"What do you mean?"

I pointed under the bed. "You told me that statue was confiscated," I said.

Ellington's eyes narrowed, and her hand let go of her braid. She leaned down and reached under her bed, and then the green tube was in the air being tossed to me. It was heavy when I caught it.

"Open it," she said.

I unzipped the bag. Inside it looked smaller than I would have thought, but empty spaces can look small. There was nothing in it. It was the perfect size for holding the Bombinating Beast, but it was not to be seen inside.

"They did confiscate it, Snicket," she said. "They took it away and left me holding the bag."

"I'm sorry," I said.

"I don't lie to my friends," she told me, and I believed her and I said I was sorry again.

"You should be," she told me. "You should trust me by now. We should be on the same page, Snicket, of the same crucial book."

She held up the book I had brought her, the one Dashiell Qwerty had been unable to deliver.

"The one that burns like a fire in the mind," I said.

"Or like a building in a town," she replied, and our talk drained away. She sat and looked at me for a minute as I listened to the rain and the night. Trying to understand Ellington Feint was like the drizzle on the window. Nothing got through. She took out the music box again, but she didn't wind the crank one way or the other.

"My father never got around to reading me *The Wind in the Willows*," she said.

"It's about four talking animals," I said.

"I usually don't like that kind of story."

"Neither do I," I said. "My sister practically had to lock me in my room to get me to start reading it."

"And where is your sister now?" she asked me.

"Locked in a room herself," I said, and then, with much more to-ing and fro-ing, we talked about Kenneth Grahame and the mole and the water rat and the toad and the badger and one thing and another. We talked a long time. Outside the window it stayed dark. Our conversation finally started to droop, and Ellington caught herself yawning and covered her mouth with her hand.

"I'd better make more coffee," she said.

"No, thank you," I said. "Don't you ever sleep?"

"Not here," she said. "Not lately. Not for a long time."

"I'll watch over you," I said. "You're running out of coffee, anyway. In fact—"

She looked at me. I can get shy in a roll of the dice.

"Snicket?"

I zipped the bag back up, for something to do, and slid it back under Ellington's bed. Then I checked if my socks were dry and they mostly were, so I slid them on my feet and then put on my shoes and tied them and tied them in double knots. "I want to ask you something," I said, when I could think of nothing else to waste my time with.

"Do you?"

"I do."

"Then do so."

"I want to ask you to do something with me tomorrow night."

Ellington smiled. "It depends what the *something* is. Is it a crime?"

"I'm sure it's against the rules and regulations of this school."

"Sounds good to me."

"I want you to sneak out and meet me tomorrow night," I said. "Together we'll go into town and go to Black Cat Coffee."

"How will we get into town?"

"In the back of a wagon," I said, "pulled by a taxi."

"Are you inviting me on a hayride, Snicket?"

"I suppose it's like a hayride."

"Just you and me, underneath the stars?"

"You don't have to make it sound so gooey," I said. "I just thought it would be a nice way to spend an evening."

"You're up to something," Ellington said. "Is this something with V.F.D.?"

I was quiet for a second. "I hope so," I said.

"OK," she said, and yawned. "I'll go. Where shall we meet—the library? That's a safe place."

"All right."

"I'll be there, with all those blank books."

"All right."

"All right, Lemony Snicket."

"All right, Filene N. Gottlin," I said. "Now go to sleep."

She frowned. "The laudanum—"

"You've had enough coffee to counteract a boatload of laudanum," I said.

"That's probably true," she said, and she let her head rest on the pillow. She was asleep in minutes. I stayed still for a moment to make sure, and then reached into my pocket and retrieved the object Kellar Haines had slipped me. I didn't know what it was going to be, but it still didn't seem right when I saw what it was.

A compass, I thought, looking at it carefully. What good are you without a map? If you don't know where you are, or where you want to go, a compass can only tell you what direction you're facing.

I leaned my head against the desk and thought. Ellington was just on the other side of a small room, but the longer I thought, the farther away she seemed. It was like the growing distance I felt inside myself, between the person I wanted to be, the brave volunteer who would soon triumph against evil treachery, and the person I was, sitting in a room with damp socks and a bump on his head, turning a compass around and around in his hands. What are you doing here? I thought. What good are you? But I did not know if I was talking to the compass or the boy who was holding it.

The black sky turned gray in the window, and I stood up quietly and looked through Ellington's binoculars at the fire pond. The surface of the water was as still as a held breath.

I rubbed my face and turned on the sink. I looked in the mirror and splashed water at my reflection, and then let the water get hot. I rinsed the cups and found another handkerchief and scooped coffee out of the flowerpot with my bare hands. I looked at the poor, sickly plant, trying to grow in the coffee grounds instead of the earth, where it belonged. I wondered what happened to things that grew up in the wrong place.

The bell rang me out of my thoughts, the sound low and loud from the nearby tower. Ellington stirred and frowned in her sleep, but it was the aroma of hot coffee that made her open her eyes.

"You made coffee," she said in surprise, when we'd told each other good morning.

"As best I could," I said.

"Thank you, Snicket," she said, and took a sip. "Your mask is in the closet, along with mine."

"Thank you."

"You're welcome."

"The bell rang, so we'd better wear them."

"Yes."

"Big day today."

"Big day today," she agreed.

"But I'll see you tonight?"

"In the library."

"In the library," I repeated, although there was something about our conversation, calm and quiet while our minds were busy and worried, that made me wonder if that was true. I swallowed my coffee the way I'd made it—as best I could. I hoped it was good enough. "I'll see you then," I said. "Unless—"

She raised her eyebrows at me. "Unless what?"

"Unless you want to tell me anything."

"Anything about what?"

"About your part," I said. "I know you're not telling me everything."

She took a long sip and gave me a long sigh. "You're not telling me everything either, Lemony Snicket. I don't really know your part, and you don't really know mine. We can only hope that our two fragments fit together. So I'll see you tonight. Unless—"

"Unless what?"

"Unless something goes wrong," Ellington said, almost in a whisper, and I finished my coffee and left her room with the bitter taste in my mouth.

Sneaking was easy business that morning. The hallways were full of masked children, walking numbly toward the front door of the Wade Academy. None of them paid any more attention to me than when I'd watched them at Stain'd Secondary School. I walked among them like I was a schoolchild too, quiet and dazed, with little idea of the treachery surrounding me. I almost envied them.

"Kenneth Grahame," someone murmured at my elbow, and I saw it had been easy business for Moxie Mallahan to sneak up beside me. Her mask sat blank under her hat, but I had the suspicion she was smiling.

"Kenneth Grahame to you," I replied, and she pulled me through one of the hallway doors. I found myself in a storage closet, lit only by a single lightbulb dangling from a worried string. The walls were lined with shelves lined with boxes. The boxes were all alike, with the word LAUDANUM stamped in silver on shiny black cardboard. The closet didn't feel big enough to hold all those boxes and Moxie and me and the masked figures of Jake and Cleo, but apparently it was.

"Good morning, Snicket," Jake said. "Take one if you need it." He held out a few pieces of rolled bark. It must be killing a good cook like Jake, I thought, to be offering such a meager breakfast.

"Thanks, but I've had my coffee," I said.

"I'll take one of those," came the voice of Ornette Lost, as she slipped through the door. "I'm feeling quite woozy this morning."

"I thought we should meet before we boarded the bus," Cleo explained, her voice muffled behind the mask. "Are we all here?"

"Not Kellar Haines," I said.

"It's hard for him to get away from his mother," Moxie said, taking a bark cigarette. "They share a room."

"Poor devil," Jake said, shaking his head.

"I agree, but there's no time to agree," I said. "There's work to be done."

"Some secret errand for V.F.D.?" Jake asked.

"In a manner of speaking," I said, a phrase which here means "No." "There's a wagon over by the gate. We need to throw it over the wall."

There was the sort of pause that occurs whenever someone says something odd and unexpected. "Our secret errand is to smash up a wagon?" Cleo asked doubtfully.

"If we angle it right," I said, "the wagon will land unharmed on something soft."

Even with a mask on her face, I could tell Moxie was frowning. "Explain yourself, Snicket."

"If we're going to defeat Hangfire," I said, "we need a fragmentary plot. That means each participant only knows his or her part of the plan. If someone's caught, they can't give away the whole show."

"Except you," Cleo pointed out.

"I'm not going to be caught," I said.

"Those are big words for someone with a goose egg on his forehead," Moxie said.

"I know you're perplexed," I said, "but we must be patient in the face of perplexity." This was something I had read in a class called Philosophy and Smoked Fish. "It's like a recipe that doesn't taste good until the last minute, or a chemical reaction that happens very gradually, or a complicated series of articles in the newspaper that gradually solves a mystery."

"A hangfire mechanism," Moxie said, and everyone looked at me.

"I suppose it is," I admitted quietly. "Now help me with the wagon and before long things will make sense."

"But how are we going to sneak off and do

that?" Moxie asked. "Stew's outside taking his guard duties very seriously."

"We need a distraction," Cleo said thoughtfully.

Ornette spoke up. "My uncles always tell me I'm driving them to distraction," she said, "so let me drive a little distraction Stew's way, once we get outside."

"Thanks for volunteering," I said. "Not just you, Lost. Everyone."

"Let's save all the thank-yous for the victory party," Jake said.

"Victory party?" Moxie repeated. "It's a little early to be planning that, isn't it?"

"Don't mind Jake," Cleo said. "He's just thinking about new recipes so he won't get scared."

"It's a good strategy," I said. "Let's all get scared later. Now let's head out."

We headed out, quietly shutting the closet door and joining the last of the schoolchildren trudging down the hallway to the Wade Academy's front entrance.

"Line up!" Stew Mitchum was barking, when I stepped outside. The rain was gone and the morning sky looked so clear that if you'd asked about rain it would have told you it didn't know what you were talking about. The students of Wade Academy were lining up on a flat part of the rocky landscape, under Stew's watchful mask. If he recognized me, from my clothing or my posture, he said nothing. He said nothing at all but "Line up!" I saw no school bus, so there was no good reason for everyone to line up. There's hardly ever a good reason to line up at school.

"*Oh!*" Ornette's cry was a piercing one, like a baby nobody likes, and she stumbled toward Stew with her hands out in front of her. "My mask is blinding me!" she cried. "I need someone strong to help me because I'm helpless!"

"Hold on there, girlie," Stew said. "Let Stewart help you." He hurried to her without another glance at the other students. Ornette continued to stumble away from us, and Stew followed eagerly.

"She's good," Moxie said.

"This is our chance," Jake said. "Let's go, gang."

We made our way right quick, ducking behind shrubs and boulders to stay out of view, clambering past the deep brick well and the fire pond I didn't want to think about. When we reached the wagon the four of us moved to the corners and pushed it awkwardly across the difficult landscape. Finally, we stood at the gate of the Wade Academy. I had us tilt the wagon as best we could. Then we threw it on the count of three. It was something to see. You have probably thrown something yourself, something unusual that perhaps you were not supposed to throw, just to see it curve through the air. It almost looked natural, as if wagons soared through the air all the time, up over a brick wall and then down, out of sight. I braced for the noise in case I was wrong, but there was only a muffled crinkling, like wrapping paper when the gift is opened. But it's not wrapping paper, I thought. What is it?

"Well, that's done," Cleo said, her voice wheezy in the mask, "although I must say this still doesn't make any sense, Snicket." She leaned down and uncurled a long piece of bark from a shrub that looked like it needed a nap. "Surely we have better things to worry about than a wagon."

"We do," I said, and then I said something I'd been wanting to say for quite some time. "Listen," I said. "None of you has to volunteer to do anything more. All of you can leave."

"It would be hard to get off the island by ourselves," Moxie said. "We might as well wait for the school bus."

"I don't mean leave this school," I said. "I

241

mean leave this town. You could walk down to the inkwells and find a ride into the city. You could hop on the train when it winds its way through here. You could even take your chances in the Clusterous Forest. You could go somewhere else and never worry about Stain'd-by-the-Sea again."

"And what will happen to the people here?" Jake asked.

"Don't think about them," I said. "Think about yourselves. All of you are very brave and resourceful people, but some of the bravest and most resourceful people in the world have come to bad ends."

There is no reason to flip back through these pages. It is true I was saying the same thing Theodora had said to me. I understood her reasons better, standing near the fire pond, dark and deep.

"Stop your nonsense," Moxie said, and the others nodded in agreement. "Tell us what's next."

"You'll have to move quickly," I said.

"Move quickly where?" Jake asked.

"To the library," I said.

"The one full of blank books?"

"You need to empty it," I told them.

Cleo crossed her arms. "What are we going to do with a bunch of blank books?"

"Throw them over the wall," I said.

Moxie put a hand on my shoulder. "Snicket, are you sure that bump on the head didn't knock something loose?"

"Leave him alone," Jake said. "Snicket's sneaky, but he's not loopy. If he says this will help, that's enough for me."

"Me too," Cleo said, pocketing the bark.

"Me too, of course," Moxie said. "I just wish I knew the whole story. I'm still a journalist, even without a typewriter."

"We'll get you a new typewriter," I said, "so you can write up the whole story, when all of this is over."

"When all of this is over," Moxie repeated quietly. "When will that be?"

"That's the wrong question," I said. "The right question is, when did it start?"

"We're the ones who ought to get started," Jake said. "Come on. We'll see you at Hungry's, Snicket."

"When the bell rings," I said, and looked up at Wade Academy. My associates nodded and turned around and went one way. I walked in the opposite direction, until I was standing under the tower. I felt a little dizzy looking up at it. Of course it's towering over you, I thought. It's a tower. You and your associates managed to distract Stew, but what about everyone else from the Inhumane Society?

For a second I thought I saw a figure, and then for a second I didn't. Maybe it was Hang-fire. Maybe it was Ellington Feint. Armstrong Feint. Sharon Haines. Lizzie Haines. Kenneth Grahame.

I breathed through the mask and stared up toward the tower and felt dizzy and perplexed and a little sick and more than a little scared. Get scared later, I told myself, just as I'd advised my associates. Get scared later, and if you're scared now remember what Kit always said. If you're not scared, she told me, it's not bravery. And you want to be brave, don't you, Snicket? Of course you do.

Of course I did, but I still felt sick. It was a sickness in my stomach and in my mouth and even in my heart. The symptoms were nervousness and dread. I don't know what the illness is called. I've had it since I was a child.

CHAPTER ELEVEN

A very long time ago, my brother and I played a game each morning while we waited for the school bus to arrive. We called the game Beethoven, and my sister refused to play because she thought it was inane. "Inane" is a word which here means that my brother and I would pretend we couldn't hear each other very well while we were talking.

"Jacques," I would say, beginning the game, "what do you think of the weather this morning?"

"Feather?" he would say. "I'm not wearing a feather this morning. This is just a hat."

"Just a cat?" I would say. "Why would you wear a cat on your head?"

"A bat in your bed?" he would say. "How terrifying! No wonder you look so sleepy."

"A book that's creepy?" I'd say, and my sister would groan and we'd keep playing until the bus arrived. Kit was right. The game was inane. But it was something to do while waiting for the bus.

It was no fun to play it by myself. I missed my brother and I missed my sister. My breath in my mask felt hot and crowded. I crouched behind a shrub and waited. Gated? I said to myself. Yes, the school grounds are gated. That's why they'll sneak out on the bus. Freak out and cuss? There's no need for panic or bad words. A flock of birds? I stared up at the sky and cut it out. It only made me miss everybody all over again. I could have snuck back to Ellington's room. I could have gone and helped my associates as they made trips back and forth from the library to the Wade Academy's front gate, doing their part in a fragmentary plot. But instead I just sat and readied myself. Everyone needs a moment on the diving board, before jumping into the depths that wait below.

I looked at Kellar's compass. It told me where north was. I thanked it very much. Instead of saying you're welcome, it told me it could also find south, east, west, northwest, and my stomach said it was sorry to interrupt but that it was hungry, and then the front gate opened and a school bus made its way across the grounds to stop at the front door of the Wade Academy, where the students were waiting. The bright yellow reminded me of two sets of painted fingernails, and sure enough Sharon Haines was driving, with Kellar stuck sitting behind her, their two masks an eerie sight in the windshield as the bus went past. I slipped out through the gate while it was still open, and walked quickly to where the wagon was waiting. There are the books, I thought, tossed hither and yon on that leafy, paper pile. But it's not leaves, is it, Snicket? It's leafy but it's not leaves, it's papery but it's not paper.

Pip and Squeak were there in the taxi, masked and ready. When you find the sort of people who will show up to give you a ride exactly when they've promised to do so, hold on to them for life.

"Morning, Snicket," Pip said. "I took the liberty of bringing you a couple of doughnuts from Hungry's, in case you hadn't had breakfast."

"You and your brother are the noblest people on earth," I said. "I was up all night without food or sleep."

"Yikes," said Squeak.

"It's OK. It was my part."

Pip tilted his mask at me. "Your part?"

"Have you read any of those mysteries," I said, "with the Belgian detective in the funny hat?"

"Of course," Pip said. "Our favorite is the

one where the girl gets murdered while bobbing for apples."

"Have you read the one that takes place on a train?"

They hadn't.

"Well," I said, spoiling the book for them and for you, "the crime turns out to have been committed by a great number of people working together. But they plotted together in such a way that nobody knew exactly what the other person was doing."

"A fragmentary plot," Squeak said.

"Precisely," I said. "I'm involved in one right now that could save a crucial aspect of this town."

They looked at each other, but they didn't need to know anything more. "Tell us what to do," Pip said.

"Do you see that wagon teetering on top of that pile of bark?"

Pip blinked. "Yes, Snicket. I see that wagon teetering on that pile of bark. If I get home to my bedroom and there's an elephant sitting in the middle of it, I'll see that too."

"Do you think you could hitch it to your taxi?"

Squeak crawled up from his position on the brakes. "We can do that."

"Then do that," I said, "and we'll load everything piled there onto the wagon."

"Everything? I think I see some books."

"Everything, including the books," I said. "We'll put the books on the bottom and that crinkly stuff on top, and let's hurry, because soon a school bus will drive out of that gate and we need to follow it to wherever it's going. Let's get started."

"We'll get started," Pip said gently. "You sit in the back and have your breakfast, Snicket. You're worn out."

I thanked them. I was worn out. I got in the back of the cab and tackled the difficult task of eating doughnuts with a mask on. It's not hard if you're not afraid of looking foolish. The one with cinnamon was my favorite. I was surprised they were as good as Hungry's doughnuts usually were, without Jake behind the counter cooking them. Perhaps I had underestimated his aunt. A cranky old woman who makes good doughnuts is better than a cranky old woman who doesn't. It doesn't excuse the crankiness, of course, but it helps. It probably helps even in Calcutta. I finished off the doughnuts and leaned back in the seat and got jostled as the brothers hooked up the wagon. You have fine associates, I told myself. Don't think about the end of the train book, when the Belgian detective catches each and every one of the plotters.

The Bellerophon brothers finished with just enough spare time to hop back in the cab as the school bus approached, its wheels cranky on the uneven surface of Offshore Island. We lay low as it passed, so the cab might look deserted to anyone looking out at it. Maybe it even looked deserted to Moxie Mallahan, whom I glimpsed as the school bus went by, masked beneath her hat and giving the cab a tiny salute. They made it, I thought. They handled the business with the books and still managed to get aboard the bus. Good people, I thought. Brave people, and I sat up carefully and watched the bus until it was a small yellow rectangle in the odd landscape of the drained sea.

"Never in my life have I liked a school bus," Pip said. "You can't get the windows open and someone's always fighting."

"You think they're exciting?" I asked, when he started the motor. "I've always found school buses dull myself."

"I said fighting."

"Something's wrong with the lighting?"

"Fighting."

"Yes, I do quite a bit of writing, actually."

The taxi turned to follow the school bus. I

heard the wheel squeak on the wagon. "What's wrong with you, Snicket?"

"Never mind," I said. "I'm worn out."

I kept playing Beethoven in my head. It was easier if I leaned back and closed my eyes. The mask rattled against the bump on my head whenever the taxi met a particularly jagged stretch of road, but other than that I felt fairly comfortable. I was more comfortable masked in the back of a rattly taxi than I'd ever been in the Far East Suite. I liked it better unsupervised. Maybe Unsupervised was my first name after all.

In my dream my sister was showing me a compass.

"Wake up, Snicket," Pip's voice said, after a while.

I woke up. "What time is it?"

"Almost one. You missed the all-clear. Take off your mask."

I took off my mask.

"That's a very handsome bump you have there," Squeak squeaked.

"It's not just handsome," I said. "It hurts, too. Where's the school bus? Did you lose it?"

"Snicket," Squeak said patiently, "it wasn't hard to follow a bright yellow school bus into town."

I looked around. The taxi was stopped in front of Hungry's diner. "Did they see you?"

"If they did, they didn't do anything about it. When they pulled to the curb I kept going so we didn't look suspicious."

"And where did they stop?"

"Around the corner," Pip said. "Right by Partial Foods, it looked like. You know that place, right?"

"I was once arrested there."

Squeak crawled up from the brakes. "What are you up to this time?"

"My fragment," I said. "My part of the plot."

"All right, then. Thanks for the tip about

the train mystery," Pip said. "I'll have to look for that at the library."

"That's exactly what I want you to do," I said. "A stop at the library and then a ride back to Offshore Island."

Squeak frowned. "Snicket, what do you mean?"

Snicket told them what he meant. They wished him luck. He needed it.

I walked around the corner with the mask in my hands, waiting for the bell. It'll ring again, I thought. Ellington will do her part at one o'clock sharp. It didn't ring, but I decided to skulk anyway, creeping around the corner so I could approach the school bus as quietly as possible.

But there was no school bus.

I walked into Partial Foods. That felt empty too, but I walked around to be sure. Stain'd-by-the-Sea's only supermarket, like the town it was in, seemed to become more and more meager each day. A barrel of grapes by the front door had gone unpurchased for so long that they were being sold as raisins. A dusty bottle of tomato juice had finally tumbled off its rickety shelf and lay spilled on the floor next to a toppled roll of paper towels. Even the vitamins looked unhealthy, and so did the only person I found. Polly Partial, the owner of Partial Foods, was in a surprised heap on the floor near the soup, rubbing her elbow and blinking around her in confusion.

"What happened?" she asked me dazedly.

"That was my question," I said.

She blinked slowly at me. "You're that Snicket kid."

"And you're that Partial lady. Anyone else here?"

"He didn't give his name," Polly Partial said, "although he reminded me of someone."

"Who?"

"Oh, it was years ago."

"OK," I said, "but what happened today?"

She gave me a shaky frown. "I had an omelet for breakfast," she said slowly, "and I sang folk songs in the shower."

"Skip to the part where you ended up on the floor," I suggested.

"He asked me something, when I'd just locked up the loading dock and was organizing prunes."

"What?"

"What what?"

"What did he ask?"

"If I had any fire. You know, for his cigarette. And then…" She trailed off and wrinkled her nose.

"And then you smelled something?" I asked. "Something sweet that made you sleepy and dizzy and of no real help?"

"That does ring a bell," she said, and then the bell rang. I pictured Ellington in the bell tower, waiting for one o'clock sharp. Maybe she'd brought a book with her, to pass the time until one o'clock. Polly Partial blinked at me.

"Just stay here for a while," I said. "The effects of laudanum will pass."

"My mask," she said. "It's over by the cash register."

"You don't need it," I said, donning mine. "Nobody does." I took one more look around the empty store and retraced my steps outside. Think, Snicket. They stopped in front of Partial Foods, but the store is deserted and the bus is gone. So whatever they want, whatever Hangfire needs them to fetch, isn't here. Then why dose Polly Partial with laudanum, just when she was organizing prunes?

The loading dock, she'd said. *Out back.*

I looked for an alley and found one, a particularly grimy one that curled around Partial Foods like something stuck to its shoe. There were garbage cans, dented and lonely, and a rat hurrying along to foil whatever treachery rats cook up for each other. There were a few doorways too dark to look through, and a child's bicycle, chained to a fence, that was more rust than transportation. I walked past it wondering where the child was who had ridden it. Somewhere else, I hoped. Nowhere near here.

The alley spat me out at the back of the building, and there was the school bus, parked at the loading dock for Partial Foods. It must have been a bustling place, back when Stain'd-by-the-Sea was a bustling town. It wasn't bustling now. The cement ramp where trucks would unload groceries was crumbling away. There were train tracks where imported foods could be dropped off, but the only train left in Stain'd-by-the-Sea would soon take Dashiell Qwerty to jail. And the loading dock itself, a raised platform leading from the tracks to the back door of Partial Foods, wasn't bustling either, although it was crowded. A line of masked schoolchildren stood still and silent, my associates among them, while the masked figure of Sharon Haines struggled with the lock on the door, using some object to try to get it open, and not using it very well. It was probably a skeleton key, I thought, a key that could open any door. But a skeleton key is like a skeleton. It doesn't do much good if you don't know how to use it. Stew Mitchum paced impatiently up and down the crumbling ramp while she struggled and struggled. He had a large black stick in his hands. A club, I thought. A cudgel, a staff, a wedge. I had a feeling it matched the bump on my head. At last Sharon Haines got the door open, and then she turned around to the students of Wade Academy and shouted something.

I never would have guessed what it was.

"Honeydew melons!" she cried. *"Grab all of the honeydew melons!"*

Stew Mitchum banged his stick against the side of the building. "You heard her!" he shouted to the people gathered on the dock. "Honeydew melons! Get moving!" He sounded as surprised as I was that the crucial item in Hangfire's sinister fragmentary plot was every sensible person's least favorite item in fruit salad.

A successful fish business, I remembered, requires loyal workers and a steady supply of food.

Sharon led the way inside, dragging Kellar as if to the dentist. The children began to file in after them, with Stew keeping watch by the door. I saw the masked figure of Ornette walk up to Stew and ask something. Ornette kept talking, gesturing wildly. Whatever she was saying was making Stew look embarrassed. He shuffled his feet. He clenched and unclenched his hands. He was probably blushing, because he looked down at the ground, and when he looked down I saw Jake, Cleo, and Moxie make their move, moving quickly, quietly, and scurrying down the alley. They were going to make it to our meeting as arranged. I thought I was probably going to be late.

The last child filed into the store, and I waited a moment before skulking onto the loading dock. They'd left the door open, but I did not need to go inside. I knew what I'd see. The last remaining schoolchildren of Stain'd-by-the-Sea would be in the produce section, stealing honeydew melons while Polly Partial lay too dazed to call the police.

And what would the police think, I wondered, if they learned their adorable son was participating in a robbery?

I found a pretty good hiding place, over by a few trash bins, and I stood amid a few disorganized prunes and waited to see what happened next. I didn't wait long. The children filed back out, holding their melons in their arms like precious bundles. As they began to file onto the school bus, I saw Ornette, holding not one but two honeydews, and she saw me and took a few cautious steps toward the trash bins.

"I might not be able to meet our peers," she murmured. "Stew is peering at me too closely."

"I don't need you to meet us," I said. "Not if you can trust your uncles."

"Doesn't everybody trust their uncles?"

"Everybody does, but not everybody should. Do they buy you popcorn at the movies or do they say it's too expensive?"

"They taught me how to sneak it into the movies under my coat."

"Then you can probably trust them. I need you to bring them a message."

Ornette shifted her melons to one hand so she could reach into a pocket and pull out another square of paper. I reached into my pocket and found a small pencil. We held out the items to each other, like matching pieces of a puzzle. It just might work, I thought, as I took the paper and wrote a few words in the handwriting I never had time to improve. You just might have the right group of volunteers.

I heard footsteps approaching just as I was done. It was too late to duck behind the trash bins. There is a walk that mothers have when they are striding angrily toward other people's children. Nothing else sounds like it in the world.

"What are you two students up to?" she asked. Her voice was buzzy behind the mask and her yellow fingernails looked chipped away. "We don't have time for nonsense. We're stealing honeydew melons."

"I'm sorry," I said, trying to sound as dazed as possible. "I got dizzy."

"Don't be sorry and don't be dizzy. Be on the bus."

"Mother," came the voice of Kellar Haines. "Leave my friends alone."

Sharon whirled around to face him. Both

mother and son were masked, so I couldn't see their faces. But we all have seen the faces of other people's families when they are fighting right in front of us.

"We didn't come to Stain'd-by-the-Sea to make friends," Sharon said. Her voice reminded me of Prosper Lost, or maybe it just sounded like the voice of every exhausted and worried adult.

Kellar Haines gave a mighty sigh, like a dam breaking. He'd been waiting to sigh like that for a long time. "*Stop it, Mother,*" he said fiercely, and took a step closer to whisper into her mask. "We can't keep assisting Hangfire," he said. "The only way to rescue Lizzie is to fight his treachery, not help it along."

The mask gasped, and Sharon raised her hand for a moment. It was perhaps the same hand she had used to strike my chaperone, but she couldn't do it again. After a pause, her shoes stalked her down the dock and onto the school bus. Kellar and I watched her go, but when I turned to see if Ornette was watching too, she was already gone.

"Thank you," I said to Kellar.

"Thank *you*," he replied. "I'd better keep an eye on my mother, though, in case she decides to warn Hangfire that some of us are working against him. Will you and the others be OK without me?"

"I think so," I said. "Will you be OK without us?"

"I'll catch the next bus into town," he promised.

"Then you'd better hurry up and join your mother."

"I'm hurryupping," Kellar said, but then he paused for a moment and looked at his mother, who was back behind the windshield. "She wasn't always like this, you know," he said.

"None of us were," I said, and let him go. The school bus started its engine as Kellar climbed aboard, and in a rising cloud of exhaust, vanishing into the sky like invisible ink, the students of Wade Academy were gone. I waited until I couldn't hear the buzzing engine, and then walked back down the alley, breathing a little easier, even with the mask on.

It came out of the darkest doorway. Most violent things do. It shoved me down and I rolled against a garbage can, losing my mask, mucking up my pants, and seriously annoying my left side. I looked up at what had happened. Stew Mitchum stood with his hands on his hips, unmasked and unpleasant. He was looking daggers at me, a phrase which here means "giving me nasty looks." I was in too much pain to look daggers back. The best I could manage was looking a couple of toothpicks.

"This is a relief," I managed to say. "You gave me a new bump instead of exacerbating the first one."

He just stared. The stick was still in his hands.

"Exacerbate," I said, "is a word which here

means 'make worse,' as in the sentence, 'Stew Mitchum is exacerbating the whole world.'"

"I don't like you, Snicket," Stew said. "I've never liked you. You're a full portion of my least favorite thing."

"What would that be?" I said. "Justice? Kindness? Literacy?"

He gave me a kick. He was good at that and I told him so, but I was gasping so much that he might not have heard me.

"You're a snoopy guy," he told me. "We don't like snoopy guys around here."

"You know what I don't like?" I said, when I was done gasping. "Suspicious fires. Enslaved schoolchildren. I don't like a town having its life drained away from it, like ink from an octopus. And speaking of sea creatures, I don't like—"

Someone cleared their throat and we both looked back at a tall, masked figure, watching us calmly. Too calmly, I thought. I wanted him worried. He gave Stew a calm wave, like a father picking up his son from school. Stew nodded and turned back to me. He stepped closer. He looked large. He smelled sweaty.

"This is your last warning," he said. He was calm now, too. "We're measuring you for a coffin. Get out of Stain'd-by-the-Sea. This town is a dangerous place for Lemony Snicket."

"It's dangerous for every decent person," I said. "Measure me all you want. Kick me around and give me goose eggs. I'm not going to stop."

Stew took one step closer, and raised his stick over his head. "You have no idea what you're doing," he told me. "This is something enormous, Snicket. It's as big as the sea."

"The sea's gone," I reminded him.

He gave me the worst kind of smile. "You're very brave, Snicket, and very resourceful. But even if you stop us from burning down Diceys—"

Hangfire cleared his throat again. Stew lowered his stick long enough for me to relax a little, and when I was relaxed he gave me one more

kick, very hard. Someone made a bad noise, a wet cough of pain. That was you, I thought. You made the noise. That was you, and this is your own blood you're tasting in your mouth.

The bell rang the all-clear. I just lay there and listened to two pairs of footsteps fading away. They're gone, I told myself. Stand up. Don't stop. You said you weren't going to stop. Don't let these criminals make you a liar.

CHAPTER TWELVE

I limped into Hungry's like a broken parade. My associates blinked at me in amazement. Even Hungry stopped wiping the wall. I must have looked worse than I felt. I felt very, very awful.

"Egad, Snicket," Cleo said, as Jake hurried from behind the counter. "What happened to you?"

"I abandoned my sister in a train station," I said.

"You're not making sense," Moxie said, and took my arm. "Sit down here."

Pip and Squeak cleared out of a booth. I sat down and leaned back. Cleo looked sharply into my eyes and then turned to her sweetheart. "Ice," she told Jake. "Ice and towels. What part hurts the worst, Snicket?"

I closed my eyes to think about this. Hungry's moved around me like a rocking chair. "All the parts I brought with me," I said, "but there are some suitcases I left behind in the city. Those don't hurt."

"Don't talk for a minute," I heard Cleo say. I felt a towel on my lip and realized my lip hurt. My own blood was still in my mouth, and I still didn't like it there. I made my eyes open and saw everyone worrying above me.

"Hungry," I said, before I knew I said it. "I'm hurt and I'm hungry."

"What's that broth you have bubbling?" Cleo asked Jake.

"Porcini mushroom," Jake said.

"Give him some," Cleo said.

Jake footstepped away and Cleo wrapped some ice in a towel and gave it to me. I held it to my side, right where Stew had kicked me, and then took the mug of soup Jake handed me and sipped. The hot broth and the cold ice worked together on me. Porcini mushrooms are rich and smooth and whispered to my body that maybe things weren't so bad. The ice was lumpy against my side and said that maybe things were bad but they would get better. I listened to them both. Hungry came over and glared at me and then looked at her nephew.

"Didn't I tell you?" she said to him. "Didn't I tell you that Snicket lad was a bad influence?"

"It's true," I said. "I am. I hope as the years pass you will find it in your heart to forgive me."

She put her rag down. "Don't get smart with me, sonny boy," she said. "There was nothing wrong with this town until you and your crazy mom showed up and started stirring things up."

A small piece of mushroom slipped down my throat. It was easier to swallow than the idea that Theodora was my mother. "There was everything wrong with this town," I said. "Things are so rotten here that even the garbage is getting stolen."

"That's true," she admitted. "I had a very nice garbage can that we kept behind the counter, but now it's gone."

"I tracked it down for you, Hungry. It's in the trunk of a Dilemma parked on Wayward Way."

She blinked. "Really?"

"Go see for yourself," I said.

She looked at me for a minute and I waited for it to work. Telling an adult to go see something for themselves always works. They never take your word for it. They always, always, have to go see, and Hungry was no different. She grumbled and she muttered and she looked at me again, but then she hurried out the door to find her garbage, and finally I could talk freely with my associates.

"That trunk probably smells awful by now," I told Cleo.

"I'll mix up a good deodorizer," she said. "Let's worry about other things."

"Like why Kellar hasn't shown up," Moxie said with a frown.

"Or Ornette," Jake said.

"Kellar's taking the next bus," I said, "and Ornette had to visit her family."

"Then everyone's accounted for," Cleo said.

"Everyone," I said, "except Filene N. Gottlin."

"Why are you smiling?" Moxie asked me.

"I guess because I'm hungry," I said. "Jake, how about lunch for everybody?"

Jake had already spooned out three more soups. "What goes great with porcini mushroom soup," he said, "is a farro risotto. Hold on, everybody."

We held on. The soup helped. Farro is a little like rice and a lot like delicious. Jake chopped onions and garlic while the farro bubbled away in a little pot, and then sautéed the whole thing up with a little cheese and served it on big round plates with a handful of fresh peas on top. If you don't like peas, it is probably because you have not had them fresh. It is the difference between reading a great book and reading the summary on the back.

"This is terrific," I said, after the first bite.

"When Cleo moved into Handkerchief Heights to continue her scientific work," Jake said, "I started growing some vegetables in the garden just outside the cottage. It's worked out pretty well."

"Let's hope the rest of the day goes the same way," I said.

Cleo frowned at me. "Whatever this fragmentary plot is," she said, "your part in it is done,

Snicket. You need to spend the rest of the day in bed."

I shook my head. Even that hurt a little. "None of us have time to lie around doing nothing," I said.

"What happened to being patient in the face of perplexity?"

"The trouble with being patient is that eventually you get tired of it," I said. "Hangfire's striking tonight. He's going to burn down Diceys Department Store. You've got to get there first and stop him."

"Burning down a department store?" Jake asked. "That's the big plot?"

"This all started with a barn fire," I reminded him, "and now they have the schoolchildren of Stain'd-by-the-Sea under their control."

Cleo frowned at me, or maybe at the cut on my lip. "But why Diceys? What's there that Hangfire wants to destroy?"

"I was hoping you might be able to tell me," I said. "What did you learn on the school bus?"

"Zilch," Moxie said. "We kept our eyes and ears open, but we learned zilch."

Zilch meant nothing. I was disappointed but not surprised. It's rare to learn things on a school bus. You can't get the windows open and someone's always fighting.

Jake sighed. "Zilch isn't enough. We can't defeat Hangfire if we don't know anything."

"Maybe it's our part not to know anything," I said, and stood up. I didn't feel great, but I didn't fall down either. "Eat quickly, everybody, and get to Diceys before dark."

"Where do you think you're going?" Cleo asked.

"I need to shower and get dressed up," I said. "I'm taking a girl on a hayride."

Moxie narrowed her eyes at me. "That's your fragment of the plot?"

"Don't get sore, Moxie," I said.

"I'm not sore," the journalist said, sorely, but then she reached into her pocket and handed something to me. I knew what it was before I felt it crinkle in my hand. It was the newspaper article I'd given her, back at the library. "I've been meaning to give you this back," she said quietly. "It made for some interesting reading."

"Really?" I said. "It's just a newspaper article. It's not about anyone you know."

She shook her head like I wasn't fooling her. "If I knew any of the people in that article," she said, "I might have hightailed it back to the city instead of staying here in Stain'd-by-the-Sea."

"And miss all the fun?" I said. "Don't be daft, Moxie." I turned my eyes from hers to say goodbye to my associates. "Good luck, everybody," I said. "I'd better get going."

"Should we call you a taxi?" Jake asked.

"No thanks," I said. "I need the walk. I need to think."

I walked. I thought. Each step hurt, and so

did most of my thoughts. I thought of a deep hole they had been digging in the city when I'd left. By now the hole was probably a fountain. People likely walked past it every day and smiled at it in admiration. Then they went to work or home or school or a restaurant or a museum or a library or any other place that brought them comfort. I tried to lay the picture of the bustling city over the sparse streets of Stain'd-by-the-Sea. It didn't fit. I was still alone, walking up the stairs of the Lost Arms. I nodded at Prosper, standing all alone in the lobby, and went up to the Far East Suite. The glitter was gone from the floor, but otherwise the place looked usual. The girl and the dog were still in the painting. The light fixture was shaped like a star, as always. And Theodora and her hair, both still in town, were looking displeased, as they generally did.

"I don't want to say I told you so," Theodora said.

"Then don't say I told you so."

"You went off by yourself, and look what happened to you."

"I'm a mess," I agreed.

"You're a bad apprentice."

"Maybe being a bad apprentice is my fragment of the plot."

She stood up and scowled. "Don't talk to me about fragmentary plots," she said. "I've been in V.F.D. since before you were born. I've been a part of ten thousand fragmentary plots all over the globe, doing my tiny part of a plan I can't even imagine. When I'm on a case I hardly ever know what's going on."

"I agree with that," I said, and headed to the shower. Theodora kept talking to me from behind the closed door, but I turned the water on and she faded to nothing. I took a long shower and got out and wiped the mirror so I could see to comb my hair. I came out wrapped in a towel and laid out the best clothes I could find. Theodora was still talking. She was talking about

Bertrand, her previous apprentice. He was a saint. He never gave her any trouble whatsoever. He was a decent person who never gave anyone reason to lose any sleep. He'd end up married to a wonderful woman and have very charming children, while I languished alone and lonely. I sat in my towel and agreed that was likely. She asked me what I thought I meant by that, and she asked other things. I gave Theodora a few answers. I gave enough answers that she couldn't say I wasn't answering but not enough answers to answer anything. I'd learned how to do this almost as soon as I'd learned to talk. Everybody does.

"Where are you going?" she asked finally.

"I know where I should go," I said. "I should go tell the Officers Mitchum to be on the alert for another mysterious fire tonight."

"Is that true?" Theodora asked me. "Do the Mitchums need to be warned?"

I sighed. "Go see for yourself," I told her. Off

she went, and I sat for a minute and then I tied
my shoes and buttoned my shirt and I gathered
up the blanket from my bed and then I gathered up the blanket from Theodora's bed and I
held them in an awkward bundle and looked at
myself in the mirror. Myself looked back. We
looked at each other for a long time.

"I don't know either," I said finally. "I don't
know if it will work," and I walked out of the
place. Pip and Squeak were waiting for me outside the Lost Arms. The wagon was still hitched
to the back of the taxi, and I laid the blankets
out on top of the papery pile that lay on top of
the books. The Bellerophon brothers looked
like they'd cleaned up a little for the occasion of
being chauffeurs for a boy taking a girl on a hayride. Their clothes looked a little less rumpled
and their hair a little less ratty. I appreciated it
and told them so. They told me the other fragments had gone off without a hitch. I said good.
We all smiled at each other for a few seconds,

and then Pip asked me the question found on the cover of this book.

I said yes.

Off we went. I didn't ride in the backseat but climbed up to the blankets and lay on my back looking at the sky. Beneath me the bark crinkled, but it wasn't bark. It was softer, and flakier, like something too old and too delicate to be of use. The wheel squeaked and the wagon swung from side to side as we headed down the street, and then swung wider as we reached the outskirts of town, and then wider still down the hill as the sun began to set. I swung back and forth like a ship in a storm, with the clouds swirling over me like the sea. The sky was still there. No one had drained it away.

I sat up as we approached the school. I hadn't thought about how to sneak back into the Wade Academy and meet Ellington in the library, but as we stopped at the gate I realized she wasn't at the library. She was on top of the wall instead, sitting elegantly with her feet dangling off the edge and her hands fiddling with her braids. She was wearing a dress that matched the color of the sunset, and she was looking down at me with her green eyes and smiling the smile that could have meant anything. Even at around thirteen years of age, I had seen many things that I couldn't help staring at. I had quite a list of them in my head. Ellington sitting atop the brick wall, smiling down at me, was now at the top of that list. It was probably at that moment that Ellington Feint ceased to be a mysterious figure in the middle of a whirlpool of difficult questions that had surrounded me since I first set foot in Stain'd-by-the-Sea, and started to become the reason I was still in Stain'd-by-the-Sea trying to answer those questions in the first place. This is very difficult to explain. It is as difficult as jumping off a wall into a wagon with scarcely enough light to see your way. But it happened anyway. Difficult things happen all the time.

She landed with a soft *crinkle* and the wagon rocked a little. Pip called up to ask if we were OK. We were. Ellington was close to me now, a little breathless from the stunt, and the fading rays of the sun shone on her freshly painted fingernails as she held the bag in her hands.

"Good evening," I said.

"It's still empty," she said, noticing where I was looking. She unzipped it to show me the empty space. It still looked small.

"Good evening," I said again.

She smiled. "Good evening. Thank you for inviting me on a hayride." She lay back and I lay back next to her. The wagon swayed, and the first insects of the evening began to whir and hum.

"It's not hay, though, is it?"

"No."

"Bark?"

"Arf, arf," I said.

She laughed and rolled closer to me. "This is definitely the loveliest part of my day."

"Tell me about the rest of it."

"I did my part," she said. "I went up to the bell tower and sat with a book until one o'clock sharp."

"What was the bell tower like?"

"Damp and unpleasant," she said. "It looks like students used to hide away from class up there, when the Wade Academy was a real school. The place was covered in old candy wrappers and graffiti from the daughters of earls and the sons of counts. *Q was here. Olaf loves Guess Who.* The view is nice, though. You can see for miles."

"But you didn't see what you hoped to see," I said.

Ellington shook her head and stared up at the sky. "I looked everywhere," she said, "from the basement full of fish tanks to where waves used to crash on the shore. My father wasn't there. He wasn't anywhere on Offshore Island. I was wrong again. Hangfire must have taken him somewhere else."

"We'll find him," I assured her. "We may even find him tonight."

She took the music box out of her pocket. "I hope so."

"Why didn't you meet me at the library? We might have missed each other."

She wound the crank and the tune began to play, tiny sounds that were still clear enough to be heard over the hum of the insects and the noises of the taxi and the squeaky wheel on the wagon. "I was wrong about that, too," she said. "The library wasn't a safe place. All the books had been removed. I don't understand it."

I shifted and the wagon creaked and crinkled under me. This meant she didn't know, I thought. This meant she hadn't been watching from the tower. Or it meant she wasn't telling me the truth. It was simple. So was the music from the music box, and I listened to it. I listened, but I still didn't know the name of the tune I was hearing.

"I've been wrong about so much," Ellington said.

"So have I," I said.

"It's a foolish feeling," she said. "I don't like it."

"Nobody does," I said. "That's why I invited you to ride on a wagon pulled by a taxi up a rocky cliff. So we wouldn't feel foolish."

She laughed, but I smiled up at the sky. A star had appeared, the first star of the evening. "What's the real reason you invited me?" she asked.

I might have been wrong once more. It might just have been the first star I could see. "Because I can't take my eyes off you," I said.

I felt her hand curl around mine. "I'm glad it's getting dark," Ellington said. "You can't see me blush."

I slipped my hand free. "That's not quite what I mean," I said. "I mean that if I don't keep an eye on you, you're likely to do something treacherous."

She sat up and looked down at me. I wondered

if she could see any of my bruises. "What do you mean by that, Lemony Snicket?"

"You know exactly what I mean, Ellington Feint. You're working with Hangfire. That's why you've been at the Wade Academy all this time."

"What?" Ellington said. "That's absurd. I disguised myself so Hangfire wouldn't recognize me."

"You changed your name and your hair," I said, "but you didn't disguise your voice, Ellington. Hangfire can imitate anyone's voice. He imitated yours not so long ago. He would have seen right through your disguise. You learned he was hiding out at the Wade Academy and went and found him. He said if you helped him he'd release your father. Of course, he'll do no such thing. Not until you give him the Bombinating Beast."

"I told you he confiscated it already."

I shook my head. "If he had it, he wouldn't keep you around, Ellington. You haven't given it to him yet. It's right there in that bag. You're afraid to give it to him because you know what he'll do with it."

"This bag is empty," Ellington said. "You saw it yourself."

"And you saw my tattoo," I said. "I learned about bags with secret compartments back in nursery school."

Ellington gave me a fierce look and unzipped the bag again. Then she reached into the empty space and pulled up a smooth black panel. The bag had a false bottom, and under the false bottom was enough room to store the object she retrieved and tossed into my lap.

"Here," she said.

The moon shone on *Caviar: Salty Jewel of the Tasty Sea*.

"It wasn't safe to keep it in my room," she said. "I didn't want Hangfire to know what I was reading and learning."

"If it's not safe for you to have this book," I said, "we should return it to the library."

Ellington bit her lip. "Dashiell Qwerty is in jail, remember?"

"Remember what you told me," I told her. "There's more to a library than the librarian. The library has a secret—an important one that burns like a fire in the mind. Hangfire wants to destroy the library so the secret will be gone forever."

"Snicket, you're wrong," she said. "Hangfire's going to burn down Diceys Department Store tonight."

"That's what he'd like me to think," I said. "I even sent my associates there so he wouldn't know I'd guessed his real plan. You were hoping to distract me tonight. Maybe we'd sit and listen to the piano at Black Cat Coffee, while this town's last hope burned to the ground."

Her eyes glistened, like tiny splashes in a deep, dark pool. "He's holding my father prisoner," she said. "What else can I do?"

"You can volunteer to do the proper thing,"

I said, with the book in my hand. Ellington did not say anything. For the rest of the ride she did not say a word, until Pip and Squeak brought the wagon to a stop in front of Stain'd-by-the-Sea's only library. All was still. No one was on the steps of the library, although there were a few shadows to be seen in the lit windows of the police station, which occupied the other half of the pillared building. At the bottom of the steps was the scraggly lawn that always looked sad, and the melted remains of a statue built long ago, depicting a war hero rescuing a kite from a tree. In a way, it was the statue that had started the fuss, as I'd learned while investigating my last big case. But the fuss had long ago grown bigger than the statue had ever been, the way an answer to a simple, clear question can turn out to be complicated and mysterious.

From the stillness came a loud rattling that reminded me of Moxie's fingers on the table, eager to type up what was going on. Then there was the whinnying of horses, and the Talkie Brothers came riding around the corner in their jalopy, raising their hands to me in a salute as it went by. They kept going. You still couldn't tell if the horses pulling the automobile were white or gray, and then they were gone.

"You see?" Ellington said to me. "There's no fire here."

"The fire department couldn't have helped," I said. "The hydrants in Stain'd-by-the-Sea have been sabotaged with some chemical. Luckily, the Talkie Brothers were warned away by their niece and are taking the night off."

"Let's take the night off too," Ellington said. "Let's go to Diceys. Let's go to Black Cat Coffee. Let's go anywhere but here. You're *wrong*, Snicket. You're wrong about me and you're wrong about what's happening."

"Let's find out," I said, and I slid down to the street holding the book. Ellington said something I didn't hear and followed me. Together we hurried across the lawn. I shouldn't let her stay with me, I thought. I should drag her to the Officers Mitchum. She's still under arrest for impersonating Cleo Knight. She's an escaped prisoner. You're running around with an escaped prisoner, Snicket. I flung open the door of the library and raced inside.

For a moment I must have looked like a hero. It was dark and I was probably a dashing figure in the doorway. But then I took two more steps and found myself on the floor. Someone had tripped me, and I'd fallen on all of the places I was already hurt. I heard something rattle out of my pocket and I felt something yanked out of my hands, and then the lights went on and some-body laughed. I didn't blame them. I was a fool-ish figure, groaning in pain. I should have been laughed at. I would have laughed at me, had I been as nasty a person as Stew Mitchum.

"You shouldn't have told me you weren't going to stop," he said, with one more chuckle just to make sure I knew he was enjoying him-self. "You told me you weren't going to stop no matter what I did, so I knew I could trip you the moment you ran in the door."

"You didn't have to hurt him," Ellington said. She was unmasked, I thought. We all were. Why hadn't the bell rung, to make it easier to skulk around town?

"What are *you* doing here?" Stew asked her.

"Never mind that and never mind him," Ellington said. "The jig is up. Snicket's figured out the plot."

"The jig's up for Snicket," Stew sneered. "The boss told me to make sure he suffered. Hangfire has a particular revulsion for members of V.F.D."

I sighed. "Revulsion" is a word which means "a vivid and violent dislike." "Members of V.F.D." was a phrase which meant Hangfire knew all along what it meant when I said I was in a kind of special program, in answer to the question

300

on the cover of this book. Who had told him? I asked myself, but Stew leaned down and waved *Caviar: Salty Jewel of the Tasty Sea* back and forth in front of my face so I couldn't think.

"Thank you for returning this book so promptly," he said. "I think I'll use it as kindling for the first match. When the Talkie Brothers get here, the chemical Hangfire put in the hydrant will destroy this place once and for all."

"The Talkie Brothers won't get here," Ellington said. "Snicket warned them away."

Stew cackled in a way that made my head hurt all over again. "You got the fire department to stay away?" he asked. "What kind of volunteer firefighter are you, Snicket?"

"Not a very good one," I said. "I'm part of an invincible army, but not a victorious one."

"I don't even know what that means," Stew said.

"That's not surprising," I said. I looked around the library for the last time. "It's not the sort of thing you learn at a top-drawer school. It means that our plans often get shattered, no matter how brilliant they are. But our purpose remains intact. We may ask the wrong questions, but we know the right answers. We might not always have an actual compass"—and here I stole a look at Ellington and then a look at the floor—"but we have a moral compass, something inside ourselves that tells us the proper thing to do."

"That's a very pretty speech," Stew sneered.

"Thank you," I told him.

"I was being sarcastic, Snicket."

"So was I, Mitchum."

"I knew that."

"Did I say you didn't?"

It was another thing you do not learn at a top-drawer school. Bickering is like baldness or lousy birthday gifts. It runs in families. Stew Mitchum was a bickerer at heart, and I was able to make him bicker while Ellington moved stealthily behind me. It was supposed to be her part, I thought. She was supposed to ring the bell tonight, but now she had another part to do. I watched her pick up the object that had fallen from my pocket and consult it, and then I watched her hurry to a certain corner of the room. If Dashiell Qwerty had told me, I thought, surely he'd told Ellington Feint about the northeast corner.

"If you don't want to argue," I was saying to Stew, "then why do you keep disagreeing with me?"

Stew cut short our bickering, something that did not run in his family. He reached into his pocket and drew out a long match. There are good fires, of course. You can't make a Hangtown fry or a porcini mushroom soup or a decent cup of coffee without fire. But the experiences I am chronicling here have left me with a permanent mark, like a bruise that never healed. You can't see it on me, but hidden in the depths of my life is the permanent opinion that a match is a wicked thing. This is wrong, of course. It's nonsense. A match is only as wicked as the person who is using it. Stew Mitchum gave me a terrible smile and lit the match by striking it against the spine of the book he had taken from me. Then he opened the book and let it drop onto its pages.

I heard the sound of a match falling onto paper. It should have been a faint crackling, a familiar noise from my school days. But this sound was different. It filled the air with a loud, shrill ringing, and then a great hiss from overhead. It was the fire alarm, and the turning on of the library's brand-new sprinkler system. Water poured down like a cloudburst. I was soaked in an instant. Everything was. Stew was soaked and the match was soaked and *Caviar: Salty Jewel of the Tasty Sea* collapsed forever into a soaked mess. Every book in the place was soaked and ruined. It was wrong to have a sprinkler system in a library. There's more to a library than the librarian, but not much more than its books. I did not know if Dashiell Qwerty had thought about the terrible effects of water when he had the sprinkler system installed, or if Ellington Feint had thought about it when she sounded the alarm. Perhaps she wanted to stop Hangfire's plan to destroy the library. Perhaps she wanted to help the plan along. I didn't get a chance to ask her.

The alarm summoned the Officers Mitchum from next door, and they hurried into the library and sputtered in the sprinklers. Theodora was next through the door. It might help you to take a moment to imagine what an onslaught of water from above did to the vast hairstyle of S. Theodora Markson.

"What's going on?" Harvey Mitchum demanded, pointing a soaked finger at me.

"Daddy!" Stew called out in his best little-boy voice. "That mean girl over there has destroyed the liberry!"

"Liberry" was a good move, I thought. It was cute enough to melt the Mitchums' heart so they didn't think to ask what their son was doing there. Instead they stomped through the stormy room and grabbed Ellington by one arm each.

"First fraud," Mimi Mitchum said to her, "and now destruction of property. You're in real trouble, miss. What do you have to say for yourself?"

Ellington stood between the police officers with her sunset dress sagged and ruined. One hand clutched her green bag, and the other clutched the compass that she held up as she looked me in the eye. It was the last I saw her for quite some time. "I was wrong," she said to me.

"So was I," I said.

The Mitchums led her out. The water kept pouring, so when we left the library it was like coming in from the rain. Theodora still looked ridiculous. She told Stew he was a hero, and he said he loved liberries more than anything else in the whole wide world. I reminded him that the library was still ruined. Every book in the place had been destroyed. Theodora said that seemed more like my fault. The Mitchums agreed but said they wouldn't arrest me. Ellington said nothing, and I said nothing to her. They took her away, and I walked down the steps. I kept my mind on looking disappointed. Hangfire was surely someplace watching. Maybe someone had given him a pair of binoculars to do it. I had to look like I had failed as I trudged to the taxi and told the Bellerophon brothers what had happened. I leaned against the wagon and sighed. I'd had a long day, rich with events, and I was in the mood to read a good book to relax. I was thinking of a particular book while I was trying to look beaten and miserable. The book is about two people who are thinking about doing something wicked. They meet on a locomotive, these strangers, and decide to trade wicked deeds. Nobody else knows what they're going to do. It's a fragmentary plot. I couldn't remember what happened next, but I knew there was a good copy of the book hidden under the hay, in the wagon I was leaning against. I thought about that and listened to the water soaking all of the blank books from the Wade Academy library. I tried to look beaten and I tried to look miserable, for anyone who was watching. It wasn't much of a disguise. I had a big smile on my face.

CHAPTER THIRTEEN

"So," Cleo said to me, "you knew all along that Hangfire planned to destroy the library."

I was having dinner with my associates at Handkerchief Heights. It was not a victory party, but still Jake had fixed the artichoke-lemon soup, with spring onions from the garden fried up as crisp as potato chips and sprinkled on top. We'd eaten the brook trout, each wrapped in grape leaves and poached with olives and rosemary, and we'd polished off the blueberry cobbler with homemade hazelnut ice cream. I'd cleared the table and Jake had made a big pot of peppermint tea—just a few springs of peppermint, also from the garden, floating in a pot of hot water—and told us, help yourself. We all helped ourselves while we talked about how we'd helped each other.

"I couldn't be sure," I said, "but I suspected as much. It wasn't enough to set those first fires and frame Dashiell Qwerty. The library had a secret—some crucial piece of information—and that had to be destroyed too, so nothing could interfere with the Inhumane Society and their treachery. And then Kellar gave me the compass, so I knew he had learned about Hangfire's plan."

"I should have told everyone sooner," Kellar said, looking around the table, "but I wasn't sure we could trust Ellington—not when Snicket said she'd been talking with my mother."

"Meanwhile, Hangfire realized that some of us were onto him," Pip said, "so he spread the false rumor that he was planning to burn down Diceys instead."

"You had us wait at Diceys that night, Snicket," Jake said, "so Hangfire would think you believed the rumor. You didn't even tell us that we were waiting at the wrong place."

"He told *me*," Ornette said, "and I told my uncles and my uncles told the horses not to respond to any alarm."

Cleo sipped her tea. "That way, Hangfire's chemical sabotage couldn't destroy the library."

"But Dashiell Qwerty's sprinkler system would have," Kellar said. "A soaked book is as useless as a burned one. But you guys switched the blank books from the Wade Academy with the real books from the library."

"*And*," Squeak squeaked, "you hid the books in plain sight, as part of a hayride you took with Ellington Feint."

The sound of typing stopped. Moxie had been working furiously on the typewriter Kellar had fetched her from 350 Wayward Way, but now she stretched her fingers and gave me a familiar look. "So your evening with Ellington was just a ruse?" she asked doubtfully.

"I couldn't take my eyes off her," I said again. I'd tried to explain Ellington Feint to Moxie Mallahan several times, and each time she gave me the same skeptical look. "Skeptical" is a word which here meant she didn't believe me. She thought I had other reasons for wanting to spend the evening with Ellington, and I'd been unable to convince her she was wrong. "I didn't know whose side she was on," I said. "I might never know. The Mitchums won't let me see her in jail, and before long she'll be on the train to the city for her trial."

"And Qwerty will be on the same train," Cleo said sadly. "We saved the library, but the librarian got a raw deal."

"You'll never convince the Mitchums of that," I said. "My chaperone tells me they received a reward for a job well done—a fruit basket from Harold Limetta."

Everyone groaned. "There are no Italian lime trees," Jake remembered, with a smile at Kellar. "Hangfire must have sent that."

"And I bet I know what kind of melon was included," Ornette said grimly. She looked tired from staying up late, nursing her uncles' wounds with the medicine Cleo had concocted, while her father worried alone in the lobby of the Lost Arms. But even tired she could fold a small piece of paper into a tiny replica of a honeydew melon.

Moxie started typing again. "Those children at Wade Academy are in the clutches of a dangerous chemical and a fiendish plot," she said, as her fingers clattered on the keys, "and too many wicked people haven't been brought to justice. The Mitchums think Stew is an innocent little boy. Hangfire is still at large. And even Sharon Haines is still helping him."

"It's true," Kellar said quietly. "I couldn't get

her to leave Wade Academy with me, even when we went into town again for more honeydews."

"You can stay at the lighthouse for as long as you want," Moxie told him, "or at least until my mother sends for me in the city. Father and I are grateful for the company."

Moxie smiled and moved over so Kellar could take over at the typewriter. It was a good friendship. It made me happy to see. The whole table was smiling, except for the girl sitting at the end. She'd always been a careful girl, so it was surprising that she had taken the risk to come and visit me. It was even riskier than it used to be. With the library soaked and closed, it was impossible to tape an article to the underside of a table. Now they had to be delivered in person.

"What's bothering you, Josephine?" I asked her.

"The same thing that's bothering you," she told me. "You might be smiling, Snicket, but your eyes are Mayday! Mayday!"

"What's 'Mayday' mean?" Pip asked.

"It's what people say when there's an emergency," Squeak told his brother. "It has a French origin."

"It *is* an emergency," Cleo said. "While we eat a fancy meal, Hangfire's still skulking around, and all those children are still on Offshore Island, dazed and obedient from all that laudanum."

"With something wicked going on in the basement," Jake said, with a shudder. "We still don't know the skinny on what's going on there."

Josephine was still looking at me. "You know, don't you, Snicket?" she said. "You know what the Inhumane Society is doing with all those children?"

I thought of *Caviar: Salty Jewel of the Tasty Sea*, the only real library book wrecked by the sprinkler system. It was my fault. I had brought it back to the library. Qwerty had tried to keep it safe. Qwerty—and maybe Ellington. Now

I'd never finish reading it. I could read all of the other rescued books, but that secret might be gone forever. "I don't know," I said finally, but even that felt wrong.

"You'll never drag it out of him," Moxie told Josephine. "Snicket still won't tell us where he's hidden all the books we managed to save."

"It's a fragmentary plot, Moxie," Pip said, without meeting my eye. He and his brother had spent a long time with me, hiding those books in an attic only reachable by a mechanized staircase, in a cupboard that was larger than it looked. Black Cat Coffee wasn't the safest place I could think of, but it was the safest place I could keep an eye on. I'd been there a number of times in the weeks since the case was closed, to sit at the counter and watch the sun rise.

"It's the wrong question," I said, "to ask what Hangfire is doing with those children."

"What's the right question?" Ornette asked, still busy with the paper. The melon flattened out and then it was a tube and then, like a miracle, it was a little statue of a lighthouse. I could almost feel it shine a light on my thoughts.

"The right question is," I said, "can we save this town?"

"Cleo's experiments are going well," Jake said quickly. "If she invents a workable invisible ink, Stain'd-by-the-Sea might rise again."

"Until that happens," Cleo said, "what can V.F.D. do about Hangfire and the Inhumane Society?"

"As far as this town is concerned," I said, "we *are* V.F.D."

Moxie nodded and brought out a paper sack, which she plunked down on the table. Inside the sack were some small cardboard boxes, and inside the boxes were business cards, one set for each of my associates. "If we're an organization," she explained, "we ought to get organized. I printed these up at *The Stain'd Lighthouse* for us to use in our official communications."

I looked at mine: LEMONY SNICKET, it said.
And below it: APPRENTICE.

"These are keen, Moxie," Jake said admiringly. "What does 'victuals' mean?"

"Good food," Cleo said, and smiled at the
word "chemist" on hers. "Thanks for this,
Moxie."

"They're perfect for discreet communication," I said. "We can't have Hangfire catching
on to what we're doing. After this dinner, we'd
better keep quiet. We shouldn't be seen together
very often, and we should communicate as
secretly as possible."

"Working together without being seen
together or communicating clearly," Kellar said.
"That'll be quite a trick."

"A fragmentary plot," Moxie said, stopping
Kellar from typing any further. "But now how
about a few rounds of Beethoven, before we go
our separate ways?"

"Desperate haze?" Kellar said. "There hasn't

been a fire in weeks, Moxie. We're not desperate
and the sky's not hazy."

"This guy's lazy?" Pip said. "How dare you
call my brother lazy! Do you know how hard it is
to work the brakes?"

"He lurks with snakes?" Cleo said. "That
sounds like a dangerous occupation."

Josephine caught my eye and gave me a signal we'd used for years to indicate that one of us
had to leave. The signal was mouthing the words
"I have to leave" and pointing to the door. I followed her out of Handkerchief Heights and into
the night.

"I'll walk you to your helicopter," I said.

She nodded, and we walked away from the
cottage. The rainy season was packing its bags
to leave, and the wind was hurrying it along.
"Tell them I said good-bye," Josephine said, with
a nod to my associates inside. "They're a fine
group, Snicket. They wouldn't let me in the door
until I said 'Kenneth Grahame.' Tell them they

seem like valuable additions to our organization. You know, I didn't even realize that apprentices were allowed to recruit volunteers."

"Volunteer means volunteer," I reminded her. "Anyone can join V.F.D."

"Not anyone," Josephine said gently. "You've let that Ellington Feint get too close to you."

"She's not close to me," I said. "She's across town, in jail."

"You know what I mean, Snicket. She's dangerous."

"Anyone can be dangerous," I said, thinking of Stew Mitchum. "They just have to end up in the wrong circumstances."

"She almost destroyed the library, Snicket."

I thought of the ruined book again. It burned like a fire in my mind. "But she almost saved the secret."

"Did she know? Did she know that was what she was doing?"

"I don't know how to answer that."

"It's a simple question, Snicket."

"Simple," I said, "but not easy. Ellington Feint is just trying to rescue a member of her family. She would do anything and everything. I would do the same if I were in her position."

Josephine stopped walking. "No, you wouldn't," she said, and reached her hand into my coat pocket. The latest newspaper article she'd brought me was folded up inside. She unfolded it, and I looked once more at the story. I hadn't read the article yet, but I didn't need to. The headline shouted THIEF! The rest of the article would just be words. The moon shone on the photograph of Kit they had printed beneath the headline. She was trying to smile but she looked grim. She was in handcuffs. Josephine's finger tapped the space behind Kit, where I recognized the two other people in the photograph for the first time.

"Gifford and Ghede," she told me, with a bitter frown. "They're two of the worst volunteers I've ever seen. They were supposed to help Kit, but they ended up making things worse."

"I'm not surprised," I said. "They tried to drug me with laudanum some time ago at the Hemlock Tearoom and Stationery Shop."

"So there's no help for your sister."

"My sister might not need help. She's very good with a skeleton key."

"If you'd gone to the city, you probably could have gotten your sister out of trouble, but you stayed here."

"My job is here," I said, looking at one of my cards.

There was a faint burst of laughter from Handkerchief Heights. "Do they know that?" Josephine asked me quietly. "Do they know what you've sacrificed to try and save this town?"

"It's a fragmentary plot," I said. "Everybody doesn't need to know."

We'd reached a large pile of crinkly material that looked like peeled bark from nearby shrubs. I'd brought it to Handkerchief Heights so we could study it further. It should be examined by a scientist, I thought. A naturalist if I could find him, but a chemist would do.

I pushed the material aside to reveal the small helicopter I'd helped Josephine hide there. I watched as she put on her helmet and checked the mechanisms one by one. She had to fly back over the Clusterous Forest, and if something went wrong she would tumble into that eerie and lawless place. Who knows what would happen to her then, I thought. And then I thought: Who knows what will happen to anyone?

"It must be lonely work," she said, strapping herself into the helicopter's only seat, "asking so many questions without anyone helping you."

"I've been a little lonely all my life," I said. "I see no reason why it should stop at age thirteen."

Josephine gave me a smile and she said

something else, but I couldn't hear it over the *skitter-skitter-skitter* as she started the helicopter. I watched her rise from the grass and mutter away across the sky. Below her the strands of the Clusterous Forest waved and wriggled like it wanted to rise up after her and bring her down. I didn't like it. I felt like I was standing on the edge of the fire pond again, on the grounds of the Wade Academy. That thing I had heard there would be bigger now, I thought, looking at the crinkly mess on the ground. It would be fiercer, if it were real.

My associate was right. The word "Mayday" does have a French origin. It comes from the term "*M'aider*," which in French means "help me." You could probably see it in my eyes as I stared out at the seaweed that lived when the sea was drained away, for no reason anyone could explain, and that moved in ways so mysterious no one could imagine them. I couldn't take my eyes off it. Help me, I thought, but I only let myself think it for a moment. Then I turned back and walked toward town. You are unsupervised, Snicket, I thought. You won't get any help. You'll have to help yourself.